Even Now

Even Now

MICHELLE LATIOLAIS

Farrar, Straus & Giroux

New York

Copyright © 1990 by Michelle Latiolais
All rights reserved
Printed in the United States of America
Published simultaneously in Canada by
Harper & Collins, Toronto
First edition, 1990

Library of Congress Cataloging-in-Publication Data
Latiolais, Michelle.
Even now : a novel / by Michelle Latiolais.—1st ed.
p. cm.
I. Title.
PS3562.A7585E9   1990   813'.54—dc20   89-25801 CIP

For Eli

Even Now

A DOOR SLAMMED SHUT at the back of the house. It was a hard, conclusive sound with no echo. She did not turn immediately to look out her window but waited the silent time she knew it would take him to cross the carpet of the long alcove, the living room, and then the entry hall. The door knocker clinked as the front door closed solidly, and then Lisa, turning her head slightly, watched him stride across the driveway to his car. He brushed leaves from the windshield with quick, swatting strokes, yanked the door open, and dropped onto the seat. He hesitated, his hands fisted on the steering wheel, and then he pulled the door closed with that gnashing sound of metal meshing with metal. He idled the car before turning it to face down the drive, and, passing, looked briefly toward her window, this briefness counter to all those times she had struggled minute after minute to see him in the cockpit of planes he was about to pilot into the air, her waving anxious—tentative—should she disturb him, distract him from the panels of switches and lights and dials, could he see her or even want to, his head and right arm now raised up, pushing toggles in the cockpit ceiling—surely now as his head dropped back down he would catch her in his vision, a smile moving his face, the hand raised to the window, the goofy flopping back and forth of his hand and then his attention drawn back into the smooth nose of plane perched above the tiny black tires.

She pulled back from the window even though she knew he could not see in, could not see her face partitioned by the geometric shadow from the leaded panes. She saw how momentary his glance had been and took this to mean something as vague and sour as the silence the carpet made of his leaving. Why had she not waved to her father, why had she not drawn the iron bolt and pushed open the window to let him know she was there, segmented by light and shadow? It was something too subtle and yet too distinct.

She told herself that she had not pulled back from the window but had remained stationary, neutral, moving neither toward her father nor away from her mother, whom she imagined in the master bedroom seated at her dressing table, her thin hands nervously still.

But she knew she had moved. She had moved away from the fisted hand at the steering wheel, away from the angry strokes at the leaves on his windshield, away from the brief hesitant glance at her window. She hadn't thought about taking sides; she did not know what they had fought over, nor had she ever really known what the quick, hissing exchanges between her parents had been about. These were tiny snakes flashing across the thatch of their days; they seemed now all of one snake which was over or behind or beneath whatever roof their experiences were becoming across their lives.

She rose from the window seat and gathered her books and the homework she had done for school about the American economy and how theoretically it was a perfectly competitive economy but in reality it wasn't perfect at all because of monopolies and government regulation and storms which destroyed crops. Weeks earlier they had studied democracy, its theories and its very different actualities. She had wondered about ideas and how they seemed to cower away from instead of control the flimsy course of days and people and weather. She pulled a cardigan from her dresser drawer, hearing the buttons click against the wood like tiny pearl hooves. She glanced at the travel clock on her desk and knew that she would be late for homeroom and that today none of these things seemed to matter: clocks, books, schedules, her teacher's punitive glance, these were insignificant, almost frivolous, as though part of a play she'd acted in long ago.

She pulled her bedroom door open and walked across the living room into the kitchen, a clean spacious room from which no smells came. Throwing her books and sweater in a chair, she walked to the refrigerator. She poured herself a glass of milk but knew as soon as its coldness filled up her hand that she could not drink it and so stood leaning over the sink tilting the glass toward the v of the carton opening. A trickle of milk worked its way down the waxy surface across the bold red print to her fingertips. She licked the droplets from her fingers; the milk tasted watery and sweet, and then it tasted like the smell of a puppy's mouth, that palatal smell both of suckling and of agedness. She heard the soft brushing rustle her mother's slip made beneath her dress, and turning, the milk carton still in her hand, she saw Elisabeth standing in the doorway smiling her cool beautiful smile.

"I guess I didn't want this milk after all," she said, looking at Elisabeth carefully before she faced the sink again.

"We're going out to breakfast," her mother said, walking into the kitchen, her heels tapping against the tile. "You can't really have anything very important to do in school today, can you? I'm starved." She wore a straight linen dress which showed her height, and sunlight through the kitchen windows glanced off the huge black buttons sewn down the side from neck to hem. "Do you want to wear something else?" she asked. "Get dressed up, have a holiday? Maybe your corduroy jumper we bought you for school?"

She returned the milk to the refrigerator; her stomach fluttered. "So, I'm not going to school today?" But she knew that, had sensed it earlier in the subordination the morning's tension had demanded of her life, her schedules. "I have a test in social studies."

"What is social studies anyway?" her mother asked. "I mean, what does one learn in social studies?"

"Mom, I have a test today."

"You can make it up tomorrow or the next day, can't you?"

"I guess so. You'll have to write me another note, though." She walked from the kitchen, leaving her books and cardigan on the chair. Halfway across the living room she kicked her shoes off and then, hooking them with her toes, flung them through the door of her bedroom, listening as they thudded against the floor under the huge rushing roar of an airplane overhead.

On her bed sat an audience of big flat eyes in round furred heads. They bobbed up and down when she sat on the bed and some then tilted left or right, their big leaning eyes implacable in their innocence. She saw them in this moment as props for that old play she had acted in, that play of schoolbooks and homework and rules that when breached resulted in little else than reprimand and the reward of having that reprimand erased from the face which had uttered it, the reward of having it so easily over and done with and entered on that long list of sweet transgressions that Lisa knew were laughed at later in life, relished even, a past world of gentle intensities—that old play in which the situation and its problems were paramount but temporary, even really, finally, imaginary.

Her world was changing and this seemed announced by the dull bell the hanger made of her closet as she pulled her jumper from the thin wire shoulders which sprang up and off the closet rod and clattered down the back wall to the floor. She left the hanger lying on the boards, its twisted wire neck rounding into a hook which circled a kitten of dust whose white grayness reminded her of a puffball she had once blown that lofted intact from its stem to the cement of the sidewalk. It had not mattered what her wish had been because as the gray fur bounced whole and gentle across the sidewalk she realized that the breath of her wish-making, its inability to shatter, had been a message, a promise of something tacit and rewarding and intact. Now, as she looked at the dust kitten within the crook of the hanger, she wished for that day when she had believed a small gray puff could forecast her future.

"Are you ready yet?" her mother asked, coming into the bedroom. "Here, come here; your collar's not right."

"I can get it."

"Okay, so what is social studies? I'm curious."

"It's not what you think it is," she said. "It's not anything worthwhile, like how people treat each other or anything like that. It's rocks. And people."

"Oh, rocks and people. A winning combination."

"Mom, you know what I mean. Geography. And then government."

"Oh, good, so they teach you about people who throw rocks. The famous rock throwers of the world. Don't you have better shoes?"

"Very funny."

"Shoes." Elisabeth walked to the window seat and, crossing her legs as she sat down, turned to look out the window. "I like this room, this seat."

"Mom?"

"I was happy when we bought this house, I thought we'd make it here. A grove of eucalyptus trees—how could we go wrong? And gardens. How can anyone go wrong with gardens?"

"The gardens are good," she said, moving toward her shoes

on the floor. "There's nothing wrong with these shoes; what's wrong with these shoes?"

" 'The gardens are good.' That doesn't even sound grammatical. The gardens are good."

"Mom, you know what I mean. I like the gardens."

"So those shoes are it." Elisabeth rose from the seat and walked around the room. She stopped at Lisa's desk and pulled open the top drawer. Pencils rolled across the bare wood. "Well, I guess we'll take all this stuff with us, huh?" The telephone was ringing in the kitchen.

"Where are we going?"

"We're going."

"We have to go somewhere?" she said.

"We're just going."

"The phone's ringing."

"I know the phone's ringing. Bring your books, you'll have some time to study. And a coat in case we're late."

"Mom, why aren't you answering the phone?"

"Because I'm not answering the phone."

"That's not a reason."

"It's an answer."

"To the phone it isn't," she said. She looked to her mother's face, to the clear, high cheekbones like two knolls on a plain at dawn; tiny mounds, she thought, tiny caches beneath a terrain of pale skin, caches of judgment and determination which to Lisa were so set there as to appear skeletal, a part of her mother's bone structure. "Who is it? Dad?"

"I'm not telepathic."

"Aren't you curious? Maybe it's not him."

"It's him," Elisabeth said. The telephone continued, and in the hollow between each ring Lisa hoped for the long, almost tragic echo that follows a telephone which has stopped ringing because no one has answered it. But the bell jingled on and she felt the crown of her head seize and constrict as though a bale of strong wire were being pulled tighter and tighter there.

"I have a headache again," she said. "I have to take some aspirin."

"You're too young to have headaches. Come on, let's go, we'll be late."

"Late for what?"

"Breakfast."

"How can I be too young for a headache when I've got one?"

"You're just hungry, sweetheart, okay? You just need something to eat." There was that breath of silence she always listened to when her mother or her father crossed the thick, soundless pile of the living-room carpet. Elisabeth was near the front door now and Lisa could hear her rummaging for her keys, the snapping and unzipping of various compartments in her purse, and then Lisa could hear the vast motionless rush of an airplane overhead mingled with the sound of her own shoe heels walking across her bedroom toward the front door and the sound of the knocker's single clink.

From the car she looked at the baby eucalyptus trees scattered on either side of the access road which led to her house. Their trunks hung with long twisted furls of bark reddish on one side and a dust brown on the other. She loved looking up into the eucalyptus trees at twilight when their sparse clumps of leaves stood against the sky like schools of tiny birds suspended and omenlike. But now the breeze tossed these clumps gently against blue sky and she saw the long green leaves—a little like the wings of a very streamlined bird, perhaps even of an airplane—as just leaves dangling from narrow branches of trees she would not be seeing much longer, trees she would be leaving soon. The Mercury reached the bottom of their road and she, along with her mother, looked both ways before Elisabeth accelerated onto the street which took them to the freeway or to the grocery store or to the private airport where she pictured her father leaning up against the slanted table studying flight charts and occasionally lifting his head to listen to some comment by another pilot just in off the runway. She pictured her father from earlier that morning, his head bent against his fist, his other hand reaching out slowly to pull the door flush with the body of the car, sealing him into the metal capsule which then slid past her window with only the sound of churning gravel beneath its four tires, and the brief glance from behind the heavy glass of its windshield. Now he was just up the street, she thought, leaning over the broad sheets of paper charting a flight, charting a direction for the plane he was about to lift into the air. He could straddle a pronged instrument across two points and start from one and arrive at the other, his sense of what would happen in a day settled, predetermined, godlike, the world and his sense of what to do with the world and how to use it acting together like birds who turn all at once in a community of direction. But she was outside this governing community, she was not one of the birds who flew with the rest, their individual wings lofting and sinking in concert with the many other sets of wings lifting and falling. No, she was outside that individual yet communal migration, outside it because she was too far inside it, being carried by it, being driven by it, inside the power of it, inside the four turning tires, inside the sloping wings, its direction very much on the outside of her, just far enough away from her to be outside her and yet all-powerful regarding her. She was inside the Mercury being taken somewhere, just as she had been inside her mother for nine months, carried along, gracefully, buoyantly, her limbs and head bobbing as the eucalyptus leaves dangled and bobbed gently from the ends of their branches, the wind powerful and pervasive about them, turning them, twisting them, lifting them up or down.

"Where are we going to eat breakfast?" she asked. From her window she could see the wooden post of a stop sign, its many crude carvings of hearts and initials. The Mercury proceeded across a wide boulevard and then up an incline toward the freeway.

"Why the hell are they still metering traffic?" Elisabeth said, edging the Mercury closer and closer to the meter, whose light flicked green and then red, allowing one car at a time to enter the ribbons of cars pushing slowly along the freeway, the ribbons breaking occasionally and then threading back together, the sun on the paint jobs making them streamers of multicolored satin. "This can't still all be rush hour."

"Maybe there's an accident or something." Yes, an accident, she thought, and the ribbons are fluttering back behind it like banners, like gift wrapping, like that ribbed ribbon you take scissors to to make long tendrils, and all these people in their cars are traveling along these narrow tendrils toward the accident, which will hunker there among the diamonds of glass and pools of gasoline as a reward, a kind of gift, for the long wait in traffic. "Mom, why do people like to look at car accidents so much?" she asked.

"This is just still rush-hour traffic," Elisabeth said. "It seems a little late, though."

"Yeah, but why do people like to look at car accidents?"

"I suppose destruction always carries some fascination."

"But why?"

"I suppose it's an accomplishment as much as casting a sculpture or making an airplane. I don't know, Lisa, you tell me, you're—"

"At school, all the girls stand around and talk about what diseases their grandparents and aunts and uncles have, and what happened to who, and how bad it was and whether they'll live or not and—"

"—and whose parents are getting divorced—is that what

you're getting at? And it's 'whomever,' not 'what happened to who.' "

"Mom, all I wanted to know was where we're going for breakfast and why people like looking at accidents. I didn't say anything—"

"Sometimes it's rude to ask questions, Lisa, sometimes you just have to let people tell you in their own time, in their own way, and I don't know why people like gawking at other people's misfortunes. Oh God, what a fucking cliché, 'other people's misfortunes'—I sound like I'm in church."

"It's all right, Mom. You wouldn't say 'fucking cliché' in church."

"Right." She rolled her eyes. "But please don't repeat that phrase; I shouldn't use language like that in front of you, and I'm sorry but under no circumstances should you repeat language you know is not polite. Okay?"

"Sure, okay, all right, but could you just tell me where we're going for breakfast?"

"We're going to the Old Clock restaurant," Elisabeth said, glancing behind her to check for traffic she would need to merge into.

"Where's that?" she asked, glancing over the car seat at the same cars her mother watched approaching slowly.

"A couple more exits. We're looking for Pinehurst." Elisabeth held her hand up to gesture "thank you" to a driver who had let her onto the freeway. "What's the word 'hurst' remind you of, Lisa?"

She thought for a moment. Hurt. First. She wasn't sure.

"Maybe you don't know the word? How about 'hearse'? You know what a hearse is, don't you?"

"Yeah."

"Well, isn't that kind of odd: coffins are made of pine and hearses carry coffins. Hmm, interesting, yes? Life's little surprises hanging over the freeway on big green signs."

"How do you spell it?"

"Hearse? How do you spell 'hearse'?"

"Yeah, how do you spell it?"

" 'Hear' and then 's,' 'e': 'hear' and 'see' but spelled with one 'e.' "

"Well, that's really weird," she said, turning in her seat, excited that her mother was playing word games with her the way she always did when she was in a good mood. "I mean, if hearses carry coffins which hold dead people and the word 'hearse' is two words, 'hear' and 'see,' and dead people can't hear and dead people can't see, then that's super-weird, right, Mom?"

"Life's little surprises. *Voilà*, Pinehurst."

AT THE OLD CLOCK RESTAURANT she watched their waitress, who had rich chestnut hair like the highly polished wood of an old desk or a fine dresser. It hung in a sheet down the waitress's back and when she stooped slightly to put down Elisabeth's coffee the sheet of hair slid as though it were all of one piece, a smooth, richly grained panel with slight variations of color. She had read once in a women's magazine that all hair colors were comprised of about twenty different colors, all combined to be either blond or brown or black. She wondered if she could distinguish twenty different colors in the waitress's hair, or whether these twenty different colors were seen only by experts or people who looked through microscopes. It was hard to see gradations of color, she thought, like the time her mother had painted a wall four times before she found the right shade of blue. At the time Lisa hadn't seen much difference in the colors, they were just four different colors, but as time went on and her mother finished upholstering the headboard and chairs that were to go in the guest room, she had seen why the other colors were "too brown" or "too purple" or "too gray." And there were the lithographs too that her mother had had matted in a blue so close to the blue of the walls that it was as though a sky parted for each lithograph to emerge and the frames hung suspended around the pictures as though they were the branches of a tree on a clear winter day.

She was thinking of those different hues of blue which had not been perfect to her mother's eye and how ultimately the color her mother had chosen had been a mixture of all three blues. The paint man, his head tilted to the side a bit, had objected vigorously every time Elisabeth approached the back counter where the paint-shaking machine stood. "Look, Mrs. Sandham, why don't you just leave that shade on for a few years, it'll grow on you. It's dove blue just like that's dove blue 'cept a little darker or a little lighter. No one will ever be able to tell the difference."

"I can tell the difference; this is too light," her mother said.

"Then keep the shades drawn. I can't keep mixing such a small order of paint, Mrs. Sandham. My boss is down on me already."

"Why should he be down on you? I'm a customer, this is customer service."

"I can't even tell the difference in these colors and I've been doing this for thirty years."

"Then you know as well as I do that colors change once they're put on walls. This has to be a bit darker, not as brown as the second one but close, and not purple like the first color. Lisa, where's that swatch of fabric I told you to get?" And Lisa had pulled the frayed piece from her pocket and spread it on the paint-splattered counter, which appeared little different from paintings she had seen in the Modern Art Museum, broad open canvases bothered with slashes and curves and drips, except now her hands smoothed the tiny piece of chintz into the lower right-hand corner like a signature, or a tiny window into a garden or an aviary where she could emerge past the red-and-black cacophony.

"This color," her mother was saying. "This blue here in this flower." She pointed with her long nail and the paint man shook his head, a look of sarcasm spreading across his face.

"Sure, Mrs. Sandham. That color. Why don't you circle it with a pen so I won't get it perhaps too orange this time. Yeah, we haven't tried 'too orange' yet."

Lisa moved away from the counter, her hands dropping to her sides; she felt sick and ill at ease. The color seemed all right to her too but she didn't wish to side with this man whose hand was angrily drawing a pen through one order and starting to write up another.

"What shade are we going to call it this time, Mrs. Sandham?" he was saying, his eyes looking out past Elisabeth into the eyes of a man waiting for service, holding a can of paint by the wire handle. "I'm open to suggestions."

The man behind Lisa gave a little laugh and then suddenly she was furious at this man waiting in line, laughing at her mother when he didn't know anything of what had gone on, anything of how beautiful her mother could make a room, rooms people walked into and sighed, gentle smiles coming to their faces. She raised her arm and swung her fist into his stomach. "Don't you laugh at my mother," she screamed. "Don't you ever laugh at my mother. Never, never," she screamed again, this time pushing against the can of paint he was holding up to protect himself. And then Elisabeth's long beautiful arms were holding her from behind, holding her fists tight against her angry chest. And then Elisabeth's torso leaned heavily against her neck and head and she felt as if she were being crushed by a lead wave.

"That kid's a psycho," the paint man was saying. She heard the sound of paint rollers knocking back and forth on a rack.

"I'm sorry," the waiting man murmured, bending down to

look into her face. "Hey, you're right. I shouldn't have been snickering. Come on. What's your name?" He knelt before her. She couldn't hear him speaking; she could see his lips move, and his worried eyes, and his big hands reaching out for her, but she couldn't hear what he was saying above the din of "That kid's a psycho, that kid's a psycho, a psycho, a psycho." She knew about kids who went insane, about that kid in the short story who waited every day for the postman's footsteps in the snow and how the footsteps became softer and softer until the boy could not hear them anymore because he was crazy. Some days she felt very far away too, far enough away to mean perhaps that she was going crazy.

"You want to finish with this order, Mrs. Sandham, so we can get on with business here," he was saying. "I suppose this man's waited long enough." The waiting man still knelt before her. She was beginning to hear the words coming from his mouth, slow, kind words which he spoke with his eyes and with his hands. "I'm really very sorry," he kept saying. "I would like you to forgive me, please. Could you do that? I don't think I can leave here until you forgive me. Please, could you forgive me?"

She didn't want this man to be kneeling on the floor in front of her, she didn't want to speak to him, she didn't know what to say to him or what he wanted really. She had only to speak a few words, she thought, but it seemed like a tremendous pressure on her. She had to push all of this away, she had to make sure that she wasn't going crazy, or that nobody knew she was, she had to hide her feelings better, she had to learn to be silent, completely quiet, like the inside of an empty church, cool and graceful.

"I'm really sorry," he was saying to her mother. "I wasn't laughing at you; I don't even know you. I'm sorry."

Her mother let go of her and, without saying anything, turned to finish with her order. The waiting man took his can of paint again in his hand and stood up. Lisa could see the brand's logo: a can of paint being poured over a globe of the world. She felt the shame of what she had just done begin to seep down over her the way the paint in the logo seeped down over the world. The man still implored her with his eyes; she felt choked by the very words she wished to speak to him, by the very words she wished to forgive him with, as though three minds were within her, one urging her to apologize so that he would not think her a stupid child, another urging her to forgive him quickly and coldly, self-righteously, and another deriding her for giving in, for not hitting him again and again and again.

"I'm sorry," she said finally, and very quietly, not raising her head to look at the man's worried face.

"You have nothing to apologize for, Lisa," her mother had said without turning around. "Nothing whatsoever."

Sitting in the booth in the Old Clock restaurant, she could still hear the flinty evenness of her mother's voice, that confidence driving through her words, coming from some place very foreign to Lisa, very inaccessible. It was a self-assuredness she hungered for. What lingered in her from the paint store was her shame; she wished to be able to scream at this shame, "No, no, I was right, I was only protecting my mother, I have a right to protect my mother, I'm not a crazy person." Her body tensed up remembering her fists driving into the man's stomach, and then that paint can with the logo of the seeping paint held out against her blows as though it meant something about her and about what she would always remember from that time, her confused self-righteous shame bearing down on her, the heavy fluid cloak which her memory would never allow her to cast off.

She wanted the beautiful hair of the waitress leaning over their table because it was not her own tangled, dull hair. She thought of walking around in this rich chestnut hair, no one recognizing her, all her past deeds assigned to someone else. She was thinking this as a man came into the restaurant carrying a briefcase. She watched him cross the floor, tall and blond and a little stooped.

"Elisabeth," he said, nodding. "So, this is Lisa. I'm glad to meet you finally." He began to sit down beside her. Her thighs stuck to the Naugahyde as she tried to slide toward the inside of the booth. It felt like huge bandages being pulled from the backs of her legs.

"Mr. Everston is my lawyer, Lisa." She pulled her leg under her on the banquette and watched the pale hair of the lawyer fall forward over his eyes, where he let it hang for a few moments before he pushed it back. He looked at her intently, holding her within his gaze for just an instant too long. She worked her leg out from under her and accidentally kicked the table pole as her shoe came down to the floor. The water glasses, the ice knocking against their sides, overflowed onto the paper place mats, leaving two deepening circles.

"How much does she know?" the lawyer said, smiling at her, weakly she thought, like a person who was not very well.

"Gene, she doesn't need to know. Custody. That's all. Just get it."

"Usually mothers do retain custody of their children in California; is there some reason he won't settle out of court?"

"Harassment." Elisabeth raised her arm to attract the waitress. She moved toward the table, pulling from her apron pocket a tablet of checks.

"Just coffee," the lawyer said without raising his head to look at the waitress. "You know what happens if you don't settle this out of court?" He turned to look at Lisa again, his gaze unreadable to her, a look of appraisal that seemed indifferent, like the way the remote-control cameras followed you in a bank. "If the judge is irate enough, he'll put her on the stand," he was saying.

"She's too young."

"It's been done." The waitress returned and, standing sideways to the table, her knees slightly bent forward, reached the large oval plate across to Lisa. She watched the waitress's hair slide across her back, the thick, shiny panel like the door to a secret passage.

"How's that?" the waitress asked, her eyes opened wide. "Think that will do you?"

"Thank you," she said, wanting the waitress to stay at the table longer, wanting her mother's lawyer to look up at the waitress as though she was there and not some wall he could order coffee from. Lisa noticed that he didn't say "thank you" or "please," and that somehow he sounded polite enough even though he was abrupt and cold. She had seen her father do the same in a restaurant and not sound rude; this was odd to her, puzzling, something that struck her as a very important detail which meant something about the world. The waitress put coffee down in front of Gene Everston. He tapped the table lightly with the end of his spoon.

"How old is she?" he asked, raising the coffee to his lips, slurping.

"Me? How old is me—I mean, how old am I?" she said, pulling strings of cheese from the omelette. "I'm ten."

"He'll do it, Elisabeth. You really want that? Think about it."

"If she has to take the stand, she has to."

"Do you know what she'll say?"

"By the time it happens, I will." The lawyer passed his hand over the cup the waitress had aimed the coffee pot toward. He started to reach down into his pants pocket.

"Forget it," Elisabeth said. "I'll get it. I can still afford some things."

"Make sure you can afford putting her on the stand."

"She's resilient."

"All children are; that doesn't make them rubber bands," he said, rising from the table.

SHE LAY PRONE ACROSS the back seat of the old Mercury, watching through a hole in the floorboard the salt-and-pepper roadbed skimming beneath her. The hole was no larger than a pencil or the circumference of her index finger, but she managed to squeeze various bits of small matter through it— a hair clip, pebbles, bits of an old gray eraser. It seemed important that she somehow connect with that speed scudding under and to the sides of her, important that she not be totally still within the capsule of speed which was her mother's car. She thought of her mother's name—Elisabeth Sandham— Elisabeth—and of her name—Lisa—caught between the "E" and the "beth." E-beth, like *E. coli*. Something she'd learned about in biology, something which ate upon something else. What was it? It didn't matter. What mattered was "Lisa" in the middle, her name, not so much mired as inescapably surrounded.

After a while she raised up her head enough to see it reflected in the chrome of the door's armrest. She observed the elongation of her eyes and of her nose. She did not so much think them distorted as changed, different, because she was different and en route to a different school and a different house.

The house in Castro Valley stood very empty behind them. She felt a slow heat come into her as she remembered the moving men maneuvering the trucks about the driveway and under the trees so that they could not be seen from the air, could not be seen by her father, who often buzzed the house when he flew in and out of the private airport nearby. The flush rose in her as she remembered the men laboring to clear the house of its contents in just under four hours. She tried hard not to think about her father, tried hard not to think about how it might feel for him returning to his home, the pots of pink and white impatiens removed from the front entry and then the umbrella stand gone in the hall, and the gallery of framed miniatures no longer above the squat credenza—that gone too—she tried not to see his eyes as they raised themselves into the hollowness of the living room. The blood pushed into her cheeks as she thought of her silence in the face of these events, a silence not brought on by horror or petrification or even sadness particularly, a ruthless silence she concluded, ruthless but in some way, somehow, demanded, insisted upon by a power beyond her though within her, controlling her.

She thought of those last moments standing in the section of her bedroom which, because of the sunlight through the leaded lozenge panes, became like a huge flat diamond shimmering. She had not said goodbye to anything, to anyone, but had just walked quickly from her empty bedroom through the wide-open living room and out of the house where she had lived for as long as she could remember. It would be her eleventh birthday soon and for a while she concentrated on this to temper the heat of her other thoughts.

"Lisa, do you know what a loner is?" her mother asked, turning her head slightly to look down into the car's back seat.

"Yeah."

"Then what is it?" Her mother's blond hair was blown back from her face as though it were a wave crashing just past her head.

"It's a car they give you when your car is at the filling station being fixed; that's a loaner." Her mother laughed slightly and then for several miles drove in silence. Low-lying fields of green stretched out from either side of the highway. The car's interior smelled vaguely of produce.

"Sometimes words have two meanings."

"Yeah. I know." She rolled over on her back and lifted her feet to the warm car window.

"Do you know the other meaning of the word 'loner'?"

"No. What is it?" She moved her bare heels together across the glass.

"A loner is a person who keeps to himself."

"Oh."

"Herself."

"Yeah."

"Who doesn't really have all that many friends—doesn't want them."

"Yeah."

Elisabeth then drove for several more miles in silence. Lisa watched her mother from the back seat: she drove with one arm stretched toward the wheel; the elbow of the other arm sat against the door ledge; her hand, the hand with the short nails, moved thoughtfully in her hair, fingering some slow mournful music, the Kol Nidre perhaps, the saddest music Lisa had ever heard her mother play. The sun was almost down and her mother's blond hair looked chestnut in the dimness. A cello case leaned from the floor of the front seat to the backrest and what Lisa could see of it was the narrow black head like a dark-haired swimmer emerging from the water.

"It's going to be dark when we get there, Mom."

"We could stop and wait for the sun to come up—"

"Yeah, let's do that, that'd be great—all those gases."

"You mean the sunrise?"

"Yeah. Dad said all those colors were made by different gases."

"Yes, he would say that." Elisabeth reached forward to pull on the headlights. Lisa knew the visibility would hardly change; it was that density of sky just before dark which absorbed light, briefly keeping it before a darker evening reflected it back. Her mother often turned the headlights on before they could be of any possible use. She heard her father's voice commenting on this, a voice that sounded to her as though it came from a dark bronze urn deep within his chest.

"Imagine," Elisabeth began. "Imagine it was something else which caused the colors. What could it be up there? Not gases."

"Yeah, it could be something else. I don't know what, though."

"Lisa, say the word 'certainly.' "

"Certainly."

"Say the word 'absolutely.' "

"Absolutely."

"Say the word 'of course.' "

"Is that one word?"

"Okay, the phrase 'of course.' "

"Of course."

"Now say the word 'yes.' "

"Yes. What are we doing this for?"

"If I hear 'yeah' come out of your mouth as an affirmative once more, I'll—"

"You'll what?"

"It sounds lazy, Lisa. As though you don't care about how you sound."

She sat up and, putting both elbows down against the back of the front seat, cleared her throat and said, enunciating each word carefully, "Of course, I care."

Elisabeth laughed gently. "Certainly, you care," and Lisa, laughing, effusive, practically stood up to say:

"Absolutely, I care."

Later that evening she awoke to the crisp, important sound of tires on gravel. "We're here," she heard her mother whisper over the back seat. "Lisa sweetheart, we're here. Open your eyes before this light hits them. Come on, little person." She could feel her mother's strong fingers brushing hair back from her forehead; she opened her eyes but she still could not see. The fingers reached deep back behind her head and lifted her. Gradually silhouettes loomed in her eyes and she saw a long dark row of trees. "Hi, Mom."

"Ready? I'm going to open this door. The light will come on." She felt a sharp draft and then another as the back door opened too. Everything was yellow, and then a back porch appeared, a door, and her mother standing there fitting a key into the lock. She watched the porch door move open and then listened to a light switch go on and off several times. "I guess we don't have electricity," her mother said quietly. "They were supposed to have connected it today."

"You can hear more with no light," she offered, stretching her legs down to the gravel, which moved like a dark tide beneath her feet.

Upstairs they unrolled the sleeping bags in the only room with carpeting, a room where the white shades pulled down over the windows glowed in the darkness. As they lined up the tops of the sleeping bags, the floor groaned beneath their footsteps, and Lisa, looking up toward the cello case standing in the corner, thought for an instant that they were three.

They ate apples and cheese sitting on the back stoop in the light from the car interior. The cement under them grew colder and colder till at last, both stiffened by the icy contact, they rose and walked again up the narrow stairs and lay down closely together, pushing the questions they knew each had to ask of the other beyond and out into the jumpy gray light of the vacant house.

"WHAT ARE THEY GOING TO ask me, Mom?" They were driving through the hills of Sonoma County, hills so dry she could hear them crackling in the hot summer sun. "Where are we going anyway?"

"Alameda. The courthouse."

"What am I supposed to say?" The Mercury slowed at the junction where the highway went either left to Napa and that valley of vineyards or west, toward San Francisco.

"Tell them the truth, sweetheart. Just do that for me."

"The truth about what?" The bright hot light of summer streamed in the car windows. She slid down in the front seat and rested her knees against the dash. She could feel the breeze from the floor vent on her legs and thighs and it seemed to her as though her body were divided, the cooled lower half roused, enlivened, the upper half hot and passive.

"Tell them you want to live with me," Elisabeth said, and then, after a pause, added: "That's the truth, isn't it?"

"That's all they're going to ask?" She moved up in the seat. An abandoned farmhouse, powdery gray in the sunlight, stood in a low field surrounded by an old truck chassis, a rusted plow, and several hutches and coops of wood the same whitish gray as the old house. A cow lay within the shadow of the truck chassis and birds lined the peak of the farmhouse roof. She noticed that the back roof of the house sloped down to one story, the same as their house did, giving it two stories in front and one in back.

"I don't really know what else they'll ask you," Elisabeth said. "You'll just have to be very careful."

"You know that old house back there—it was shaped just like ours."

"They're called saltboxes."

"Why do they call them that?"

"Lisa, I don't know about any whys today. Just stop asking me. Tell the judge you want to live with me and get it over with."

GENE EVERSTON CAME quickly up to the car as Elisabeth paid the lot attendant the all-day fee for parking. He tapped his knuckles on Lisa's window for her to unlock the door and then, pulling the door open, slid briskly in. She scrambled toward her mother on the car seat. "Elisabeth. Lisa. Look, we've changed plans. She's to be seen in the judge's chambers with both lawyers in attendance. The judge won't put her on the stand. It's better this way. Only one snag, though. We won't be heard until afternoon and Mandauer has requested that his client have lunch with her. The judge agreed."

For an hour Gene Everston, Elisabeth, and Lisa sat in the back row of the courtroom. Lisa could not see much of the proceedings of other cases, but she heard the mood of the room change from very quiet and still, with one voice speaking solemnly, to loud and active, with people standing, chairs and shoes scuffling on the floor, and voices raised in either indignation or congratulation. She looked around as best she could for her father. Several people close by moved magazines or papers back and forth, fanning themselves in the warm still air of the courtroom. Occasionally, her mother and the lawyer leaned across her to whisper something; she heard snatches of words, "custody," "child support," "visitation rights." They were words which seemed similar to "allowance" or "doctor's appointment," words whose ramifications seemed technical, logical, even simple because they had a ring of the inevitable about them. The courtroom became very quiet while a voice announced that the judge would recess for a half hour. Lisa heard her last name announced twice. *Sandham* versus *Sandham*.

"This is better, Elisabeth," Gene Everston whispered. "He won't get to talk to her at lunch." They both rose and Lisa looked up at them an instant before standing up. She felt her mother's hand on the back of her head and she turned to see her smiling as though through a thin veil of moss.

"I'll be right at the door when you come out," her mother said. "I'll be waiting for you."

"Where's Dad?" No one answered her. The lawyer reached his hand back around her shoulder and, bringing her even with him in the aisle, pressured her firmly toward the double doors and out into the broad hallway. He said nothing to her as he walked her through a single wooden door, down another hallway, and then into a room lined with books with red and black bands across their bindings. A hat rack with one empty coat hanger stood behind a square wooden desk surrounded by chairs. She rubbed her cheek to remove the rough feel of the lawyer's coat, which had brushed against her as they walked down the hall. She felt afraid of something; she didn't know what it might be. The room was too quiet; nothing seemed to move in its yellow-brown light. She thought of the soundless carpet across the living room in Castro Valley, of the tiny flashing snakes she had so often imagined there, their hissings always beneath the day-to-day existence of her life and of her parents' life. Her stomach fluttered against her rib cage. She saw the lone coat hanger in the sallow light and it was a snake, its head pulled back ready to strike. Her stomach flew out against her rib cage again; it felt like a bird she had seen drunk on pyracantha berries flying over and over again into the reflection of trees in a plate-glass window. Gene Everston smiled at her through the lock of blond hair which hung over his steady eyes. A door opened and then a man in robes was stooping down to her, smiling, patting her shoulders.

She couldn't read the careful smiles. They weren't the obvious, broad smiles people usually gave children—they weren't animated, charitable; these were smiles of a different order, elegant and insincere, powerful, as though they were decrees sent down from a great distance.

Mr. Everston introduced her to the judge and then to a Mr. Mandauer, who came into the room through the same door that she and her mother's lawyer had. The judge pulled chairs out into the room. There were three in a semicircle and then one backed up against a long library table piled with papers and books. The judge directed her to sit in this one and she did, feeling the cool leather touch the skin at the backs of her knees.

"We are here to determine which parent your custody will

be awarded to," the judge said. "Both Mr. Everston and Mr. Mandauer are going to ask you some questions." She twined her ankles together and heard the heel of her shoe kick backward into the chair leg. She looked down into her lap and was surprised to see her hands fisted, with the thumbs sticking through between the index and middle fingers.

"Lisa, are you happy living with your mother?" Mr. Everston began.

There was a long silence and then she answered, "Yes."

"Do you think that you would like to go on living with your mother?" Mr. Everston said, looking through the lock of hair hanging in front of his eyes. She nodded her head.

"Lisa, have you ever lived with your father? Just your father and you alone?" Mr. Mandauer asked. She looked up at his small head and the thin gray hair smoothed down over it.

"No."

"Isn't there the possibility that you would like such an arrangement?" Mr. Mandauer continued. She moved her head up and down in agreement. "Has your father ever mistreated you?" She shook her head quickly. "Can you say beyond a shadow of a doubt that you wouldn't want to live with him?"

"No," she said hoarsely.

"Nor has your mother ever mistreated you, has she?" Mr. Everston asked abruptly.

"Doesn't your mother tend to take you out of school frequently, Lisa?" Mr. Mandauer asked.

"Sometimes," she answered.

"Doesn't this make it difficult for you to catch up with your schoolwork?"

"Not really."

"Oh, come, Lisa, aren't you behind? Don't you like school?"

"I like it."

"Then certainly being absent so much keeps you behind the other children; you mustn't like that."

"I don't know. I don't think I'm behind."

"Does your mother leave you alone at night or on week-ends?" Mr. Mandauer asked. She shook her head slowly.

"But you have been left alone at night before when your parents were still together. Isn't that so?" Mr. Everston asked.

"They said they trusted me. I didn't have to have a babysitter."

"Was this your mother or your father who trusted you?" Mr. Mandauer asked, moving forward in his chair, his small, close face looking straight at her. "Wasn't it your mother who suggested you were old enough to take care of yourself?"

"She trusts me," Lisa said, the heel of her shoe lifting and kicking back hard against the chair leg. "I don't—"

"Wouldn't you feel most comfortable living with a person who was there when you needed him?"

"Mr. Mandauer," the judge said, the coat hanger just above his head, a thin black snake bowed back, about to strike. Who would you rather live with, Lisa, they all seemed to ask at once, your mother or your father? Her knee throbbed from kicking the chair leg.

"Lisa, you are a very lucky girl. We are giving you a choice. Few children are given this opportunity," Mr. Mandauer said.

She held her arms tightly crossed over her chest; she tried to keep from bunching her fists up into her armpits. She didn't want to appear like a child. Her parents trusted her. She wanted these men to understand why, to see that she was grown up; she wanted them to see why her parents trusted her. But they didn't seem to really be paying attention to her, they had those smiles, those faraway decrees written across their faces. They kept saying she had a choice, that she could choose between her father and her mother.

The yellow-brown light of the room seemed denser. For an instant she could not see their faces. It was silent for the longest time. She kept hearing them say that she had a choice, and hearing her mother say to just tell them that she wanted to live with her in Sonoma.

"Neither your mother nor your father is here, Lisa. You can say anything you wish to say. They can't hear you," the judge said.

"I like living with my mother but—"

Mr. Mandauer sat back briskly in his chair. "That doesn't mean, though, that you wouldn't like living with your father, does it?"

"No. I liked living with my father," she said, her stomach flinching hard against her ribs.

"All right, gentlemen. I've heard enough," the judge snapped. "Mr. Everston, remain a minute. Mr. Mandauer, you can take her to her father. They are to eat lunch together."

She followed the lawyer out the door and down the hallway which led onto the broader hall. It was filled with people standing, conferring in serious close groups of two and three. She watched the back of Mr. Mandauer's gray head move back and forth in a gesture of saying no and then looked past him to see her father standing across the wide hall, his eyes intent on his lawyer. She wanted to run to him across the marble floor, she wanted to see him and to talk to him after so many months, to be aloft in his arms again, weightless. Instead, because his face was tightening, she backed up against the door just closing into the jamb and felt the knob at her shoulder blades, the knob pushing through her chest. She watched him now standing with Mr. Mandauer, his hands at his waist so that his blazer lifted back off his hips. He looked thin to her and his face moved almost imperceptibly as his eyes caught her standing across the broad hall backed up against the door. He said something brief to his lawyer and walked to her, his face not moving, his eyes very steady, not dark, she thought, not angry. She hugged him as he leaned down to her. His cotton shirt felt damp and hot and something made her pull gently away from him; it was a sharp smell, the smell of the peccaries at the zoo, the funny boarlike animals with the high smell of dirt and wet dog and something musty she couldn't name. He took her hand, and his palm was also damp; she felt mean and she didn't know why, and then sheepish for not wanting to touch him, for not wanting him to touch her. They walked to an elevator, where she watched his long arm reach and press the call button. A red light came on over their heads, a bell rang, the doors slid open, and a policeman escorting a handcuffed man walked past them. She turned to watch over her shoulder the tan, muscular arms bound at the wrists. She heard the soft chink of the metal chain as the two men disappeared down the broad hall. "Lisa," her father said softly. He stood with his back against the elevator door, which banged into him like a robot and then receded with a whir. "Don't stare."

They were alone in the elevator and he turned to face the panel of buttons. He pushed the top button and without turning to her said, "There's a cafeteria in the building." The doors rolled shut and she felt the same dense, yellow-brown light of the judge's chambers closing in about her. She watched her father's heavily veined hands; she listened to the steady whir of the elevator as it rose through the floors of the courthouse; her mother hadn't been waiting, hadn't been in the broad marble hall at all. She was down below, she thought, somewhere amid the groups of conferring people and the man with handcuffs and the policeman; she was somewhere not near the door where Lisa had stood with the knob in her back. And now, as the elevator rose higher, Elisabeth was even farther below. Lisa pictured the great cement skeleton of this building being built, the huge open shelves draped here and there with cables like long black hairs; this courthouse had once looked like that, she thought, had once been unfinished, gaping, useless and silent. Workmen had finished it, though.

They had laid the halls with marble and the walls with grained panels of wood; they had glazed the windows and hinged the doors. She knew there was no use in wishing the world were different, in wishing that this building had never been built. She consoled herself by imagining the elevator a metal fist encasing her, punching her through the courthouse's ceilings and floors, punching her through metal and wire and cement, and out into the soft shapeless blue sky where she reached with her shoulders for a branch, reached as though she were swimming the butterfly, reached for a branch and then another and then a higher one.

"I'm sorry you didn't want to come live with me," her father said, putting both his hands at his hips, looking down at the floor. She felt her shoulders still reaching, her shoulders up close around her neck, their tension solid as a heavy coat; she had known this was coming, known from the moment she saw his face across the hall, his lawyer shaking his head back and forth, his lawyer telling him she had not wanted to live with him, that lie she was sure his lawyer had told in the din of all those people talking in huddled groups of two and three. She looked up over the elevator doors and watched the floor numbers change from three to four and from four to five. Her father stretched his entire hand across his face and held it there till the elevator doors slid open with a chime. His hand fell slowly from his face and then he placed it across her forehead and drew it back through her hair and down her neck to the small of her back. She felt her forehead wet with his tears, and when he nudged her gently from the elevator she could feel his tears cooling against her skin, above her eyes.

They pushed through the cafeteria line, sliding the orange plastic trays down the stainless-steel counter, their hands reaching uncertainly for small bowls of fruit and cottage cheese and salads of macaroni and pickles. Neither of them reached for a piece of fish or a hamburger patty being dished up from the steaming rectangular pans. She looked at the hands of the cafeteria workers in clear plastic gloves as they gripped long shiny spoons dripping with cheese sauce or thin brown juice or shreds of spinach and onion; she looked at their hair flattened down under clear plastic caps, and the long indentation the elastic made across their foreheads like the furrow a stick would make drawn across a patch of sand. She felt very uncomfortable, this brightly lit scene before her, the light glinting off the plastic and the stainless steel and the grease in the food, and then her father moving slowly alongside her, barely speaking, a word here or there to point out a fresh vegetable or a tiny loaf of corn bread, but not whole sentences or even whole phrases. She wanted to tell him many things, but she didn't want to tell him in front of all these people, she didn't want to cry here near these lights that were making the skin on her hands look mottled and raw. She searched for something to say to him, for some subject that would draw him away from the sentence he had spoken in the elevator.

"Why, if you eat desserts at the end of the meal, are they at the beginning of the line?" she asked finally, her voice a surprise to her, sounding not at all like her own, but like her mother's, the words edged with Elisabeth's mixture of bemusement and disapproval.

Her father looked at her. He seemed for a moment happy, and then the smile faded and he told the cashier to put both trays on one check, that they were together. He held the smooth leather wallet that she had given him for his birthday, the wallet made of lambskin that felt like butter. It fell open in his hands and he pulled the mossy bills from its folds and then returned it to his breast pocket. The motion of lifting the lapel of his blazer off his chest to push the wallet down the inside pocket was always beautiful to her, a cool elegant working of the hands that was so very different from any movement she or her mother ever made. The cashier handed him some coins and he stacked them on her tray, his fingers shoring them up as though they were poker chips.

It was an old habit, this giving her all his change whenever he received it, or when he came home in the evenings, his trip to her bedroom to drop whatever coins he had acquired during the day down the thick neck of the blue glass water jug that stood in her closet. "The fur coat fund," he called it when he spoke to her in private, "the college fund," her future, her education, when Elisabeth was around.

Lisa watched his back as he carried his tray out into the clamor of the cafeteria dining room. He stopped for an instant and stood very straight, surveying the room for a table, and then continued on toward a back wall hung with pictures of almond orchards and old buckboards and men with watch chains festooning their thick wool vests. He put his tray down and then turned and looked for her across the wide room. She looked down so that she would not catch his gaze and then made her way across the linoleum floor with her shoulders and arms very stiffly holding the tray, her eyes intent on the tall glasses of water and milk which slid slowly on the smooth surface. Then she looked up and he was there taking the tray from her.

"We're over here," he said, walking away briskly.

The room was vast and loud to her as she moved through the tables and chairs filled with people talking and eating, the silverware clashing like an army of tiny swords being wielded, parrying and jabbing and thrusting. Her father was taking glasses and dishes from the trays and setting them on the table. He put the trays in front of the salt and pepper and sugar, leaving the stack of coins on the wet orange plastic where he had put them moments earlier. "You took your college fund when you moved," he said, sitting down, reaching for a packet of sugar.

"I thought it was my fur coat fund," she said, anxiously sure that this was an easy subject, a secret between them they both relished.

"Oh, I'd say your mother has won that one too," he said.

She felt the clamorous room close in around her, and her father with his words pushing her deeper and deeper into a dark shroud or cave where she would live from here on out, the huge noise about her and over her always, but also oddly away from her because she could only pay attention to a different war, a different battle, one already fought for her, one she'd been a part of but only vaguely, peripherally, like a mascot.

"Dad," she began slowly, "I didn't say I didn't want to come live with you. I never said that."

"You said what your mother told you to say—eat some lunch."

"No, I didn't."

"All right, then, you said what the lawyer told you to say." He spread his napkin in his lap and lifted his fork and then put it down with a snap; the sound speared her ear as though it were a thistle impelled there by a strong wind. "You couldn't for once in your life have disobeyed, could you?" he said. "You couldn't have said you spent most of your life with me anyway while your mother was off playing the fucking cello with a bunch of overweight penguins, could you?" She watched him lift his fork once again and hold it suspended over his food. Her chest felt as though there were a fist inside her punching out against her stomach and rib cage.

"Daddy, I didn't say anything that anybody told me to say."

"That only makes it worse, Lisa. That means you said it on your own."

"But I didn't say anything." The fist was in her neck now, closing up her throat, suffocating her. "What did I say? You keep saying I said something. I didn't." The fist had turned to water now and it poured from her, drowning her in the middle of all these people with their tiny swords flashing back and forth, stabbing and plunging and talking as though nothing in the world was wrong. She dropped her forehead against the metal lip of the table and felt the tears fall into her lap and then rise again as the fist—the fist pressed against her back and chest and lodged up into her throat. "What did I say, what did I say, what did I say?" she pleaded from the darkness beneath the table. "I didn't say anything. What did I say?"

There was a moment, suspended, inert, and then she felt the table move slightly as her father turned to her. "Baby, I'm sorry, really, I'm sorry. These bastards tell you things. They think it will make you feel better—make you feel as though you haven't wasted your money on them." She could feel her father's hand on her back, the solid weight that spread out through his fingers as though his hand were a starfish holding to a rock. "Lisa, come on, look at me." He tried to raise her face with his other hand. She smelled his cologne, that scent like a walk in brisk fall air with someone's fireplace burning oak logs.

"I didn't say anything," she whispered.

"I know. Forget it. We'll make the best of things." He moved the dish of grapefruit sections closer to her, and then pulled the cottage cheese in too. "You'd better eat something. My visitation rights will be revoked if you don't." There was anger in his voice again; she felt a vague exhaustion as though she had dreamed about something terrible all night and was now awake, slowly remembering the details. She looked across at his untouched food, the bowl of pale macaroni salad, the shredded red cabbage with slashes of carrots. He was thin. His eyes were quiet, unhappy.

"You should eat too," she said. She watched him pick up his fork and move it into the shreds of cabbage. He looked out across the cafeteria, chewing; his dark hair reached down the collar of his shirt and she missed seeing him come home in the evenings, his tie still held by the shirt collar but loose, unknotted, the narrow strip of silk running the length of his chest like a priest's tippet.

"So," he began. "I suppose you in fact know why they put desserts at the beginning of cafeteria lines."

"I asked you," she said. "I don't know why. I just thought it was funny."

"It is funny," he said, laughing and then sighing. "But why the hell would you notice something like that? What possible reason could you have for caring about a detail like that anyway? So what. They display desserts first, then you get fruit, then shit, then more shit. Who cares." He turned and looked down at her. His eyes were unreadable now, dark, impassive.

"It just seems kind of the opposite of what it should be, don't you think? Desserts at the beginning instead of the end." She thought of a painting she had done of her father many years ago, a painting that her mother had framed and hung in the living room. Lisa had rendered him carefully, the dark hair, the brown, almost black eyes, the heavy brows. She had worked from the memory of his face one day on a beach in Kauai in the late afternoon. She traced his cheekbones and forehead very precisely, their dark tan against the heavy sunlight, and then, to everyone's surprise but her own, had painted his chin blue, the dark indigo blue of the Pacific just before a storm. His chin had been blue in the deep sunlight of Hawaii, and it was blue now in the fluorescent lighting of the cafeteria. Her mother called the painting "Bluebeard," and Lisa knew that that was someone who killed his wives, but she hadn't meant any of what her father and mother had liked about the painting; she saw his strong, heavy chin as secretive, as dark, a place where some providence was which she would never know. It was partly his beard growing through, yes, but it was more. "Dad? Do you remember 'Bluebeard'?"

"Thanks. Now I really know whose side you're on." The words came fast and sarcastic; she hadn't thought quickly enough, hadn't realized what he could make of her question. "What about it, Lisa?" She couldn't answer for a moment, couldn't find the air in her lungs to push the words out into the room.

"The painting, Daddy. I meant the painting."

"I know you meant the painting." She almost asked him why. If he knew she meant the painting, then why would he deliberately misunderstand her? She almost asked him, but then something stopped her: she hadn't seen the world as nonsensical; she had seen it as completely reasonable, as completely plotted out, something her parents seemed always to know about, the complexities, the subtleties. And she had assumed that the way she saw things was as subtle and complex and reasonable; she had forgotten about deliberateness, about anger.

"You thought it was strange, at first, that I made your chin blue, but then you and Mom didn't think it was strange. You had some reason for it, and you liked it."

"So?"

She began to think that asking certain questions was childish, infantile, an indication that she, Lisa, didn't have a clue about the world. She told herself she had to think now, she had to figure out what mattered. It was something in the eyes of the lawyers, something she couldn't articulate, and something too in her father's eyes, their solid, impassive darkness. The answer, she thought, was behind the vague exhaustion she now felt in her shoulders and jaw, an answer that wasn't an answer at all but a dark envelopment that became an answer, her answer, in that it directed her, led her, kept her captive within a form of movement: a hard, choking apprehension of the world.

"It doesn't matter, does it?" she said to her father. "It doesn't matter why."

"No, it doesn't matter. There's no matter to what matters," he said.

"Sounds like a song," she said.

"A very bad song. Eat that lunch or I'll have to take you somewhere decent and then I'll be arrested for kidnapping."

"How could you be arrested for kidnapping?"—the question out of her mouth before she could stop it. "You're my father."

"Why aren't you living with me? You're my daughter; you get the picture." She put a grapefruit section in her mouth and the sourness of it seemed to make the section grow so that her throat didn't feel large enough and she had a hard time swallowing. She reached for a sugar packet and ripped the tiny strip of paper from its top; the sugar was white and then clear and then invisible as she sprinkled it across the remaining grapefruit.

"You didn't have to get divorced, though—" She pulled another packet of sugar from the container in the center of the table. Mr. Mandauer's wiry body moved in and around the tables and chairs, working his way toward them. "There's your lawyer," she said, a wave of anger cresting in her, black and gray and cold.

"Herb. Here." Her father raised his hand. "Have a seat." She watched the lawyer pull a chair out with one hand and slide the trays down the table with the other. He didn't look at her. She felt as though she were about to hate him, and then, almost inexplicably, she felt appreciative of his coldness to her, his aloofness: he didn't care about her, wouldn't care about her: she had merely been a temporary obstacle for him. Yes, it was true, she had made him lose his case, but still, as her father had said, Mr. Mandauer had gotten paid for his work; she couldn't hurt him—couldn't hurt him as she had hurt her father. She almost wanted to thank him. He remained, and would always remain, Mr. Mandauer, a man with a small head and thin gray hair, and an unalterable face and heart and soul. In fact, she almost loved him. He had taken her father's side, had cared about her father and what he, Neville, wanted. And he had done the right thing by turning her father against her: she didn't deserve anything from her father, didn't even deserve to have little secrets with him anymore. She had betrayed her father, and Mr. Mandauer had merely made that clear to him in the broad marble hall of the courthouse echoing with other people's claims and defenses. She pushed her food away and waited.

In the courtroom she sat on the aisle. She leaned out so that she saw the low gate, the judge's bench, and her parents' lawyers standing together in their dark suits facing the judge. The three of them spoke quietly together and then a commotion started and her mother squeezed her knee. "Let's go, honey," she said softly, tucking her handbag under her arm, smiling, a lilt coming into her voice. "We have our lives to get on with."

As ELISABETH AND LISA came off the freeway onto Franklin Street in San Francisco, Lisa watched the apartment houses they passed, the different foyers, some marble-floored, some protected by wrought iron, some mirrored, reflecting back the passing cars. Up ahead, the hands of a clock on the stone face of a church's bell tower read two-thirty.

"Well, I think we deserve a little something for our efforts," Elisabeth said.

"Why don't we just go home, Mom?" She looked down a wide four-lane street to the tall buildings of downtown San Francisco cast in a clear, glasslike light. She knew she should feel excited, that the city was beautiful and full of possibility and movement and a certain type of density that she could lose herself to. Any other day she would have felt exhilarated to be here, the descending and cresting movement of the car on the streets thrilling her, the twirl of excitement spiraling through her stomach and chest and up into her cheeks and eyes. Any other day, the brisk air of the city would have moved across her face like a gesture, a beckoning.

Today, she did not roll down the window to feel the breeze off the bay; she could not seem to infuse energy into her arms and hands. She looked across at her mother, whose face was mottled with shadows which came from the sunlight shining through the leaves of the elms that lined the street. She could feel her mother's excitement, her happy anticipation of an afternoon spent in the city.

"What do you want to do?" she finally asked. She thought of the bead store they went to sometimes, and of the plastic trays with all the little compartments that they would then fill with tiny orbs of amber and glass and crystal. She heard the quiet clicking sound the beads made in the tiny compartments of the trays as she and her mother moved about the shop leaning over the wide, bead-mosaicked counters. She thought of the restaurant down the alley in Chinatown with the carts of miniature steaming dishes, the shrimp balls, the parchment-wrapped chicken, the taro root which, deep-fat-fried, looked like hedgehogs.

"We're going to celebrate, honey. Come on, you're mine, that's worth celebrating."

She rolled gently into the door as her mother turned the car up Sacramento Street.

"Hey, sit up, sweetheart. See that house with the lions, that's where Sir Arthur Conan Doyle's brother lived. Conan Doyle would come to visit and he wrote some of the Sherlock Holmes stories there."

"You've never told me that before," she said, a little spike rising in her. "Why haven't you ever showed me that before? We've been to San Francisco a lot."

"Can't show you everything all at once; you'd be bored."

Her mother read street signs, her face craned up against the windshield. "How would I impress you on future trips?"

"Mom, pay attention, you're going to hit that car." The Mercury jolted backward. "I told you, I warned you."

"Oh Christ, Lisa, shut up; it's only a little love tap. Why do you think cars have bumpers?"

The car ahead pulled just around the corner and stopped. A man in a business suit got out and walked to the rear of his car. He kneeled down and looked at the bumper and then stood leaning up against the trunk, waiting for Elisabeth to pull up behind him. "Wait here," she said, pulling the emergency brake tightly. "This will just take a minute."

She could see the man's face just above the windshield wiper, its stern exasperation softening as her mother approached his car. She ducked her head a bit to peer through the wedge of glass between the wiper blade and the dashboard. Their faces were turned away now but she could see her mother's arms outstretched in an expression of "Who knows how I accidentally tapped your bumper?" and then they both were laughing, the man propping his shoe on his bumper so he could use his knee as an armrest, and Elisabeth taking his pen to lean against the trunk of his car and write something on a piece of paper he handed her. They seemed to be talking now about something other than the car. The man pointed to a row of narrow little houses across the street and then gestured at the Mercury. Her mother put her hands on her hips and tilted her head to look downward. She then raised it sideways and shook it gently back and forth. Now the man had his hands outstretched and they both were laughing. Lisa raised her head to look over the wiper blade again. Her mother and the man appeared farther away now that they were in the bigger frame of the entire car window. She lowered her head again to look through the wedge of glass created by the wiper blade and the horizon of the dashboard. The narrow sliver of glass was a focus, she decided, like the focus hands created cupped around one's eyes to keep out the glary sun.

The man in his black business suit and her mother in the linen dress with the short jacket were still talking. Her mother's stockings sparkled in the sunlight, as did the reflectors on the man's car. When Lisa raised her head above the windshield wiper the sparkles went away; it was a different picture, farther away, bigger and duller. She lowered her head again; the wedge revealed a glint of gold near the man's hand. At first she thought it was a pen, and then she saw it was a ring with stones which caught the light. They were shaking hands now and she straightened up in the seat as her mother walked back to the car.

"Okay, let's go." Elisabeth tapped the horn ring a couple of short toots, waved at the man, and then accelerated on down the street. "Look for, oh, never mind, there it is."

"What happened?" she asked.

"Nothing happened, we exchanged addresses, he showed me where his offices are located."

"What's he do?" she asked.

"He's a doctor."

"He had a diamond ring on," she said. "I could see it sparkling in the sun."

"So," her mother said, smiling at her. "What of it?"

"You told me once that you didn't like men who wore jewelry."

"I said I didn't like the look of jewelry on men, not that I didn't like men who wore jewelry."

"Why'd you talk for so long?"

"We didn't, Lisa. Two minutes have elapsed since I got out of this car. Two little minutes. What are you, my mother?"

"Yeah, sort of," she replied.

"What does that mean?"

"You don't have anyone else to take care of you now except me. Right?" she said. "So, I'm kind of your mother."

"And my father and my husband, too. Horrors. I'll never get to do anything fun. You're an old fuddy-duddy."

"I am not."

"Tight-laced as they come. Reactionary even. That's how children are."

"What's that mean, reactionary? Whatever it means, I am not."

"That would be my definition of children: whatever they are, they're not."

"Dad didn't wear jewelry."

"Could we not talk about your father for a few days? I know that's not a fair thing to ask of you, but I'm a little Neville'd out at this point. And anyway, your father did wear jewelry when I first met him. Okay?"

"I'm sorry."

"You just don't have to get so upset about things. Take it easy. I'm not going to get us killed and I'm not going to marry a man I rear-ended on the day I divorced your father."

"Sure," she said quietly.

Her mother pulled the column shift into reverse and started backing the car into a parking place.

"That's the vaguest damn word, 'sure,' " her mother said, leaning back across the front seat to see.

"I didn't mean it to be vague."

"No, no. Vague is good sometimes, very good. I understand from Gene that you were somewhat vague today; that's good, the judge thought you were confused."

"I don't remember being confused," she said. She wanted the car to stop so that she could pull the handle and push her shoulders against the door and feel the cool, brisk air wash across her face and eyes. She knew her mother was angry at her for not telling the judge what she had told her to tell him. She sensed her mother wouldn't come straight out and say it;

that wasn't her way, and besides, her mother wanted to celebrate, to have a good time, and Lisa didn't want to spoil that,
didn't want to spoil the best mood she had seen Elisabeth in
for weeks. She didn't remember exactly what had been said
in the judge's chambers. She recalled being very nervous and
then feeling angry but unexplainably so. She felt the faraway
exhaustion seeping in behind her eyes: obviously, her mother
knew all about what had been said, obviously she would remember the conversation her lawyer had related to her, even
if she, Lisa, didn't. What *had* happened, she wondered, what
had been said? She felt trapped in some sort of careless world
where what she said meant something completely different from
what she thought she was saying—what others thought she
was saying. "I wasn't confused at all," she continued. "I answered the questions, that's all."

"You did a good job, baby. Thank you." But she could still
feel something between them, as though they were folding
long sheets and one kept folding one way and the other folded
the sheet in another way, and every time Lisa brought the
sheet together the way she thought her mother was folding,
her mother would be refolding the creases to be straight with
what Lisa's had been previously.

"They didn't ask what you said they'd ask," she said. "At
least, not for a long time. They asked about babysitters."

"It doesn't matter now," Elisabeth said. "I don't really care
anymore; you're here, that's what counts."

"But you think I said something wrong. You just said that—
that I was vague. I wasn't vague. I answered the questions."

"Lisa, what do you want to do today? Hmmm? I drove here
because there's this good consignment shop."

"I want you to believe me. I wasn't vague, I answered their
questions. I didn't say anything wrong."

"Who ever said you said anything wrong, Lisa? Hmmm,
who? Let's drop this and have some fun."

She couldn't break out of the world where what she said

became something very different from what she meant. She thought the lawyers, the judge, her parents, looked at her as though she were behind several windows of glass, and they waited on her, on her words, and when she had spoken some they seemed to cheer or shout or argue till her words were transformed before her into some language she did not speak. Individually or collectively these people would scatter before her on their several and various missions, using her words as their banners. All she had said was "sure" and it became "vague"; she had said she "liked living with her mother" and that had become she "didn't want to live with her father"; she had said she felt as though she were a mother in some ways to her mother and that had become something about children being false. It seemed there was no breaking through; she was enclosed in a vessel of windows.

She looked up the narrow Victorian building to its eaves. Pigeons rested in the large white curls of gesso and wood. She heard their tremulous murmurs as though they were the soft sweet sounds one hears below the surface of still water. Her mother walked ahead of her up the steps and the sound of the pigeons disappeared in the shrill tinkle of the bell attached to the consignment shop door. Three floors loomed before them of old clothing and velvet hats and champagne glasses etched with roses and crumb waiters with their brushes worn and hatboxes stuffed with embroidered cocktail napkins. The shop smelled of perfume and old wool. It smelled good to her, like the smell—she supposed—of grandparents. She wondered what having grandparents would have been like. Would their houses have contained a similar teapot or the picture of a young President smiling? Would her grandmothers have looked like the ladies behind the glass counters, white hair swept off their softening faces, eyes slow behind tiny folds of skin, their hands fluttery? Would they have left her a long strand of pearls like the one looped deeply down the mannequin standing in the window wearing a plumed hat stuck through with diamond-studded hatpins?

She had seen pictures of her grandparents, small pictures that her parents called black-and-white but which to her were more the color of tree bark against an overcast sky. There was also the picture of her father's father's car smashed into a pine tree on a mountain pass, and always the story that came when the picture was shown of how he had jacked the car up in order to change a tire and how the car had rolled off the jack and across his face as he had tried to hold the car in place. She knew her grandfather had once been a fine speaker, a public man, but after the accident, because a bridge rested where his front teeth had once been, a bridge which clicked when he spoke, he had retired to his den, where he read thick volumes of ancient history and drew pictures of automobiles as half monster, half machine, furious incarnations of tires rounding down into claws which spread across the ground like the thick exposed roots of a tree. She had never seen these drawings, though she turned for a moment thinking that they must be hanging behind her on the high white walls of this house where people's pasts were sold.

"You were certainly lost for a second, weren't you?" her mother said, holding a pale yellow dress out to her. "What do you think of this? It's beautiful wool."

She was off guard and it took her a moment to focus on the column of small pearl buttons down the front of the dress to its drop waist. "Here, try it on. There's a dressing room back there."

She passed behind a curtain patterned with huge red flowers. The fabric did not reach all the way to the floor and she could see the shoes of people moving about the shop. The dress felt scratchy against her skin and smelled of dry-cleaning fluid, that non-smell, she thought, that smell of nothing and no one. The dress made her feel like a doll. It was pretty and her pale brown hair fell down around her shoulders like corn silk.

"Come out and show us," her mother called through the curtain. Lisa crooked her arm over her shoulder, reaching to find the zipper pull. The yellow wool bunched around her neck and chin; it prickled as though her face was deep into a bush, trying to smell a flower. She kept straining to get the zipper up. She felt ridiculous and desperate. She couldn't go out there without the dress closed discreetly around her body; she couldn't seem to maneuver the pull which locked the tiny metal teeth together; she heard in her mind: whatever children are, they aren't. She didn't know what that meant; she wanted to be safely within the dress.

Her stomach grumbled and she knew it was from hunger and yet she wasn't hungry for food; she wanted the good empty powerful feeling of deprivation—which was completely within her command. The growls moved in her stomach, deep and resounding and vigorous. Today, for the first time, she loved this feeling, the hunger pangs rumbling at the base of her spine, under her heart. She felt a new vitality in herself, an assurance, her body—her body within the dress—independent and sovereign.

She had caught hold of the zipper. She was pulling the tiny metal teeth together, each metal tooth finding its partner— the narrow metal mouth closing up her back slowly. She dropped her arm and her shoulders fell too. She could still feel the bristle of the wool against her chin and neck.

"Come out and show us," her mother called again. "How long could it possibly take you to try on a dress?" Lisa looked at the powdery back of the fabric curtain. She turned in the mirror—the yellow dress turned, its short skirt falling from the drop waist in pleats. She tried to focus on her face in the mirror; it blurred before her as she turned, and she turned again, the weight of her head falling backward, spinning, her chest leading. She couldn't stop, she couldn't see herself in the mirror, the image was obscured, she kept turning, sure she could finally capture herself there in the glass, there in the silver surface. Then, though she had not noticed before, she realized her eyes were filled with tears, sharp, stinging tears that pushed their way out of her eyes and, once on her cheeks, cooled from her body spinning in the tiny room— cooled and tightened there as though they were strings constricting around her face, pulling it into itself like a net closing on its catch as it is hauled in and onto the planked deck.

"Stop twirling." The curtain rings clattered and smashed against the wall as her mother pulled the huge red flowers aside. "What are—what's wrong, sweetheart? Oh, baby, I'm sorry, whatever it is, I'm sorry." Her mother held her closely within her arms, and then straightened and turned to pull the curtain closed around them. "Here, let me see this and then we'll go. We'll go, okay?" Lisa felt very calm, as though she were in a cool dark room alone. She stood away from her mother in the cramped space and smiled. "I don't know why," she whispered, half laughing. "I don't know why I was crying. I'm happy, Mom, really I'm happy," she said in a higher-pitched voice. "I love you." Her mother pushed her hair away from her face and back off her shoulders. She looked up into her mother's eyes and felt guilty at the look of shame she saw there. "Really, Mom, I don't know, I was just being a baby. This dress is kind of scratchy."

"It's too big anyway. Here, turn around." She faced the corner of the dressing room and could smell the chalky plasterboard of the wall jutting out on either side of her nose. Her mother's hands moved at the back of her head. "You did a good job on this one; your hair's all caught up in the zipper. We might have to cut this." Lisa reached her hands behind her back and started to pull. She wanted out of the dress; she felt its wool against her skin more acutely now; it was warm, prickly, and she began to feel the closeness of the room. The room became the elevator in the courthouse, the same dark dense light, and her father standing above her, crying, his wet hand finding her forehead as the doors chimed open, and now her mother was there, pulling at her hair in the zipper, now Elisabeth was there though she had not been earlier, had not been waiting for Lisa outside the judge's chambers as she had promised she would be.

"Stop it, you're hurting me. I'll do it myself." She was angry. She pivoted her back around against the wall. The hairs being pulled pierced like pins going into her scalp. She reached her hand back and ripped the hair from the zipper; she hated herself. She twisted the back of the dress around to her face and grabbed frantically at the small metal teeth holding the lock of her own hair. She felt brutal, as though she could run her fist through the wall.

Her mother drew the curtain after herself. She hadn't said anything or looked back at her. Everything was very still, even the shoes and ankles of people browsing the shop that she had been able to see below the curtain had ceased moving. She hated these people for not continuing to move about her. She didn't want to be able to stop them from doing whatever they had been doing; she didn't want that power—and she hated them for giving it to her.

The yellow dress slid down off her waist and hips and pushed a breeze about her legs. This movement reminded her that she and her mother were going to leave, and she wanted to leave, and also that she wanted to stay in San Francisco and drink green tea from tiny cups with no handles; she wanted her father to be angry with her because she deserved it; she wanted him to forget that she had ever existed, to forget that he had a daughter—maybe, she said to herself, he would get married and have a good daughter, one who loved him and wanted to live with him always; she wanted to love her mother as a queen would love her, graciously, acceptingly, generously, sternly; she wanted to be alone in the field behind the house in Sonoma, the wild wheat reaching up into the palms of her hands, the kerneled tips springing back up behind her as she moved, her path obscured before she could turn to see where she had come from.

ELISABETH PULLED THE MERCURY alongside a fire hydrant, pushed the door open, and then turned to her. "Come on in with me and pick out what you want."

"This is an illegal parking place," she said.

"We'll just be a minute."

In the liquor store she reached through the strips of plastic hanging over the refrigerated section for a can of cola. Behind her, her mother selected two stemmed champagne flutes from a rack and walked to the front of the store. Lisa heard her ask for a pint of Tanqueray and a small bit of ice.

"I don't want a huge bag. I just want enough for these two glasses."

"Who's drinking the gin?" the man behind the counter asked. Lisa watched him lean his hands on the cash register, his broad chest like a life jacket around his body.

"My eleven-year-old. She's had a rough day." The man, expressionless, pulled a roll of paper towels from beneath the counter and started to wipe out the glasses.

"It's not a good idea to drink while you're driving."

"It's a great idea. The best I've had all day."

"Okay. Your choice of weapons." He moved down the counter and back behind a curtained doorway. Elisabeth drew two pieces of beef jerky from a jar and was twisting the lid on when he returned. "You need a lemon or a lime?" he asked, setting the glasses on the counter filled with ice.

"No, the ice is great. Thank you."

He raised one of the glasses over his head to read the price tag and then rang up the gin and the cola Lisa had placed on the counter. He slipped each glass into a narrow bag made for wine bottles and put these bags and the drinks in a larger bag. "Hold that upright," he said, handing the bag to her. "Your mother's going to be pretty upset if you spill her ice." He smiled at her and she liked his broad chest leaning across the counter, its robust strength easeful to her as though here was another man who could never be hurt.

She placed the bag on the floor of the car, her mother telling her to wedge her legs against it. "We'll get into that after the bridge," Elisabeth said, and then hesitated, her hand on the keys in the ignition. "We're going home, sweetheart—okay?" As she straightened up in the seat she pulled Lisa's face toward hers and kissed her on the forehead. "We're going home."

"I'm sorry about not wanting to—"

"Hey, let's forget it. I was wrong. I was only thinking about myself. Let's go home."

"Mom. You were trying to buy me a new dress; you weren't just thinking about yourself."

"Let's drop it. It doesn't matter anyway."

"It does so matter. It really matters."

"Maybe. Maybe not. What matters is vastly ambiguous sometimes. And wisdom about it won't get you shit in this world."

"Mom, you've got me."

"That, I'm not ambiguous about. But I can't speak for you."

They slowed through the toll gates and paid the uniformed woman standing in the metal reinforced cubicle banded round with strips of red reflectors.

"What a job that woman has," Elisabeth said as she accelerated up the low ramplike incline onto the bridge. "Of course, she's got a great view." They passed under the high red towers with the heavy suspension cables swagged on either side of them. "When I get tired of seeing this bridge, perhaps it will be time for me to die." Her mother looked out through the cables to the ocean and the sun low in the white sky.

"You'd better not get tired of seeing this bridge, then," Lisa said.

As they were coming off the bridge and up the grade nearing the tunnels, she began to rustle in the bag for their drinks. She poured her mother some gin and handed the glass to her across the seat.

"Good girl. Keep it low," Elisabeth said, glancing in the rearview mirror. "Turn around. Look at that light casting off the stucco and tile. Hurry, look," her mother said again, but the darkness of the tunnel had already enclosed them and she listened to the noises of the tiled darkness, that noise she heard as the roar of engines on a wet night.

"Honk the horn," she said. "Come on, Mom, honk it," and she half reached over to do it herself because her mother was in the process of transferring her glass to her right hand, which held the wheel. But Elisabeth pushed her wrist into the horn ring and pressed once and then again. The blast of the horn echoed in the tunnel. It sounded desperate, lost—she didn't know why people honked horns in tunnels—she thought to herself that she would never ask for it again. She bent over into the dark well between the dash and the seat; the paper sack rustled; there was the pop and sigh of the soda can she had opened, and then as she poured the cola into the glass the tunnel ended and the light of Marin washed down over her back.

"Mom, I'm kind of tired," she said. "Could you hold this while I get in the back seat?"

The back seat seemed airy and spacious and almost like a separate room. She started to stretch her legs out across the seat.

"Hey, wait. You can't have a nap until we have a toast. To my baby girl, whom I love very much."

They clinked glasses low over the wide car seat, the clear

gin and the russet cola swimming together for an instant and
then washing back apart into the blinding bright sunlight of
two glasses catching reflections.

"It's bad luck if you don't drink after a toast," her mother
said. "Come on, drink up. You need the liquids anyway."

The cola tasted watery and was almost clear as she poured
the rest of it slowly down the hole in the floorboard, her fingers
holding the ice in the glass so it wouldn't chime. She tried to
push one of the cubes down the hole but instead had to watch
it melt and then be sucked clear as though it were a bubble,
which in shrinking had finally burst and was then gone, leaving
only a moist residue.

SHE AND HER MOTHER had lived in Sonoma almost five years, and in a matter of weeks it would be her sixteenth birthday. She waited through the summer not so much for her birthday as for the festival, sewing every day on a black gown she was making to wear to the dress ball, a function that was new on the event roster. She did not know how to sew but had figured it out as she went along, buying a pattern here for a long wide skirt and there for an off-the-shoulder top with cupped sleeves. She bought yards of lace with the design of garlands and yards studded with tufts of velvet, and tucked and gathered these long strips until the effect was bountiful and Victorian and beautiful to her. On evenings through the summer she lit candles in her bedroom to work on the dress, the light casting across the black moiré like moonlight on a dark lake.

Recently she had started to smell the must from the winery down the street, its first harvest in, the fermentation already begun. She could hear the trucks thundering to the winery, to the huge stainless-steel vats, and from the winery, back to the vineyards of Glen Ellen or Schellville or Kenwood. On these evenings as she sewed she thought of the Vintage Festival, of Sonoma's annual fete to celebrate Bacchus, though here within the town square Bacchus, or the Bacchanalia, became what her mother referred to as "catholicized." There was no frenzied cacophony of horns to resemble goats or bulls, no gods torn limb from limb to be scattered among the vines for fertilization, no bull slaughtered and carried to the revelers to be eaten raw. Here on the ground where the Bear flag had first been raised, its bottom strip of red cut from the petticoat of a prostitute who serviced the Spanish troops barracked along the square, she watched a whole steer turn and roast slowly over a charcoal pit the size of her bedroom. She tossed potatoes at salamis hanging from a scaffold, and won glass figurines, a giraffe with amber ears, a snake clear as water; she wandered past booths selling hats and pottery and jewelry; she watched people eat roast ox and corn and French bread from sturdy paper plates, and, to the even strumming of guitars, she practiced the nonchalance of people at a fair in autumn. On Sunday, the last festival day, she had watched now for several years the ministers from the Congregational and Episcopal churches dress as Spanish padres and bless the fanned baskets of grapes set out under the tile and adobe eaves of the old mission. Each time she felt transported to another era, as though she were an Indian girl sitting in reverence through a ceremony bestowed upon grapes no bigger than blueberries.

She watched other pageants too: the reenactment of the marriage of one of General Vallejo's daughters, a costumed affair in which all the women wore the high mother-of-pearl combs draped with mantillas of Valencienne lace, and the men wore silk hats, dove morning coats, and slim-fitting slacks which were caught by a strap that reached down under the instep of pointed, highly polished boots. And after the wedding, after a wave to her mother, who played the cello for the ceremony, she would saunter over to the gunslinging pageant, to Gino's restaurant, which served as an old Western brawling canteen. Men rolled off the tiled roof firing six-shooters and landing astride horses hitched there at the ready, their harnesses dancing with Mexican silver. Over the years she had stopped flinching at the gunshots, but she could never relish the sight of the horses' backs dropping sharply as the men landed on them from the rooftop.

Finally festival weekend came, and early that Saturday morning as she walked down East Spain Street toward the plaza, she saw street sweepers like armored cars parked just to the side of the mission. She saw groups of policemen setting up cordons, talking solemnly through walkie-talkies, and reaching down their indigo legs to clutch the blackjack or holster, to joggle it back and forth slightly, a reflex motion, she supposed, to adjust or to assure the façade of security. It made her think of the morning of her twelfth birthday, when she ran down the hall through the streaming sunshine toward her mother's bedroom, toward her mother's bed, which she bounded onto, throwing her head down against the pillows nearest the door, those her mother did not use, hitting her temple down against the cold metal butt of a gun which sprang up at her face as she recoiled, the tears beading in her eyes at the same stammering rate as the realization beaded in her brow—of the gun, its reality, its hardness, and what a weapon implied, perhaps even indicated was present.

She crossed the street just before the mission and walked under the balconies of the Blue Wing Inn, walked past the dry wooden posts furled with stalks of corn husks and runners of red and brown and golden grape leaves. The antique shop inside the inn looked dignified and undisturbed by the goings-ons outside its windows, windows she always looked at closely for the many tiny bubbles within their thickness, windows she loved because they were of glass made before technology, before perfection became the joylessness of mass, machine production. She saw the bubbles in the glass as somehow compassionate, charitable, a surface which had absorbed humanity, much the way a table worn by hands is bowed and hued by lives which it has served. She looked through the bubbles to a Regulator clock leaning on a table up against a wall; the metal pendulum swung back and forth and its face read 8:30.

She hurried on to the bakery to get bread and a pull-apart cake before the bakery vestibule clogged with tourists and locals alike wanting the famous bread, wanting the Gallic air of walking with a long loaf of bread tucked beneath the upper arm.

As she rounded the corner she could see that the four streets which squared the plaza were cleared of cars but were not yet filled with festival-goers. She could see the men from the Rotary Club setting up the salami throw near the tiny library which sat within the plaza. The Rotarians, dressed like singers in a barbershop quartet, with black armbands and frilled shirts, bantered back and forth as they lifted boxes of salami from a truck backed up to within a foot of the stand hung with red, white, and blue bunting and the Rotary wheel symbol. A group of women dressed in long flowered skirts of calico with matching sunbonnets were talking with one another, each occasionally turning from the group to watch a child of theirs or to answer a call from a husband or a greeting from a friend.

Through the bakery window she saw Mrs. Armstrong waiting amid nine or ten people. She held a gray slip of paper with a number on it. Lisa pushed through the glass door, ringing the bells attached there as she entered.

"Hello, Mrs. Armstrong." She had met her only twice before and now it seemed so long ago, the two years more like twenty. She thought of David holding Elisabeth by the waist, and her, Lisa, by the shoulders while he introduced his mother, his tall elegant mother: "This is Louise Armstrong—or, in the vernacular, my mother." She had kept repeating the word "vernacular" over and over in her mind so that she could look it up when she got home. She remembered his ease, the sense of possession in his voice, the pride he obviously felt in holding Elisabeth to his side—it seemed so long ago, miragelike, and complicated, something being acted out behind a frosted window, something that had at first seemed simple, natural, a man, someone to be with Elisabeth.

But it had suddenly become something else, suddenly and without warning her mother, arms akimbo, had stood at the foot of the stairs demanding, "Have you been on my bed?"

"What do you mean 'have I been on your bed'?" she had replied, not paying much attention.

"What have you been doing on my bed?"

"Mother, I have no idea what you're talking about—what is this? The Three Bears?"

"That's exactly what I mean—who has been on my bed—who have you been with?"

"You've got to be joking. I haven't *been* on your bed. I don't think I've even *been* in your bedroom. What are you—"

"Do not use that tone of voice with me, missy." Her mother took her arm and steered her toward the living-room sofa. "You're going to sit here until you tell me who you've been with on my bed."

"This is crazy. I haven't been on your bed. I can't believe how paranoid you are. I can't believe this." And then her mother's voice faltered.

"Has David been over here?"

"No one has been over here today," she said, her voice quiet and even. "I haven't been in your bedroom. One of your students called, a John Adams, says he needs, oh, that! *There*, I was in your room to answer the phone. Now are you satisfied? I sat, *sat*, on your bed to answer the phone."

"You're not supposed to answer the phone in my bedroom and you know that."

"Mother. That's absurd. Why can't I answer the phone there? Why do I have to run all the way downstairs, possibly break my legs doing those stairs, just to answer the phone in a room that's not a bedroom? Be reasonable."

"If I ever catch you on my bed again—"

"What do you mean 'again'—I can't believe this—I fucking sat on your bed to answer the telephone so that one of your pimply music students could complain about his audition."

"Don't go into my bedroom. That room is off limits. That's final."

"Nothing is final about an accusation. Don't accuse me of some fantasy of yours and then because it's not true think that I'll forget the accusation." Her mother looked at her, an unhappy confusion in her eyes, and then slowly turned her face to the window.

"You've got to learn to hold something back, baby." Elisabeth's back slackened; the tension dropped from her shoulders. She looked down at the palms of her hands, curling the fingers toward her, studying her nails, the short, squared-off set of her left hand and the longer, tapered set of her right. "Hold something back," she repeated.

And then David was gone, his house rented to other people, his little red car in his mother's carriage house on blocks, his name hardly spoken, his mother a ghost along with him, but here now, standing in the bakery.

"Hello, dear. Lisa, isn't it?" Mrs. Armstrong said.

"Yes. Lisa." She moved to pull a number from the dispenser near the door.

"Did you know that David is back from Saudi? He's finished what he calls 'The Shipwreck of the Desert.' We must see you and your mother later on, at the ball perhaps. But your mother will be playing at the wedding, so we'll see you there, won't we?"

"Number forty-two."

"Here," Mrs. Armstrong said, handing her slip up to the woman dressed all in white, like a nurse, her gray hair pulled back into a net, a tiny silver cross hanging almost to the ribbed white fabric of her collar. Lisa looked past the customers and over the counters for Mr. Bouchard, the baker, who had once, it was rumored, been baker to the Grimaldis. He allowed no woman who worked for him to use scented soaps, to wear perfume, or to smoke. The old baker claimed the scents could flavor the delicate *sacripantina* he made with the cream filling and the cream dome on top. She couldn't see him among the tall steel cooling racks.

"Number forty-three."

The door chimed open with a new customer and tinkled shut after Mrs. Armstrong. Lisa waited, being pressed closer and closer to the spotless cases filled with trays of napoleons and croissants and madeleines and almond crescents and harvest tarts of fig, prune, apricot, and blackberry. A tall case of round cakes, their tops peaked high with billowing curls of chocolate and cream, was directly in front of her. She could smell their cool, sweet cream, and behind her the pungent odor of patchouli; she could smell the soft dust of flour and meal, and to the left of her, the scent of lavender bath powder. She thought of David back from Saudi Arabia after two years— those years behind her quiet, uncomplicated with any memory of him, only with that calm, blunt absence he had left.

"Number forty-four."

A tall woman with braces on her teeth ordered a dozen blueberry muffins, and for the first time in months Lisa allowed herself to think of her father. *Daddy, what is blueberry, what does it taste like?* And he had answered that blueberry tasted like lemon and cherry and celery—tasted different but good, and that she, Lisa, his little 'Lisabeth,' would like the flavor.

And she had liked the flavor, liked the round berries popping in her mouth, their lemon-cherry-celery flavor smoothed by the crème anglaise which floated around them in the goblet, and had liked her father, her father there watching her, his gold signet ring going up and down with the thin cigar he smoked with his brandy, the brandy he drank all through dinner, hardly touching his food. She had been wearing a silk voile dress with pink satin roses and formal waiters had moved about them, slicing her filet into small bites, replenishing her father's brandy, changing the silverware, lighting her father's cigars, and then the oldest waiter, the one who wore shoes like velvet slippers and moved very slowly, the one with the shock of white hair, had brought a telephone, a telephone right up to the table, and her father had instructed them that he would take it elsewhere, not at the table, and then her mother had appeared seemingly from nowhere, standing over her, the look of angered concern on her face, the look of possession and of militancy there showering down on Lisa as she lifted the last spoon of blueberries, the sauce touching her lips and running down her throat, down to the place where her father now resided, where he lived so vaguely and quietly, that father of the past who she knew had loved her. Through the visitations of the last five years she and Neville had hardly spoken to each other, and though the silence had not been from anger, she wished in ways that it had been. At least anger finally exploded and was gone or, at any rate, subdued. Instead, the silence between her and her father lingered, high and sickening, like the smell of a decomposing animal.

SHE SAT ON THE BENCH before her mother's dressing table, careful not to catch on the drawer pulls the jet beads which she had strung to hang in garlands from her dress. Cast against the wall were odd shadows from a swagged lamp with one entire petal of its tulip design missing. It hung, on its good days, with this defect to the back, but her mother was forever climbing a stepladder and rehooking the chain link because some force in the house, some gravity, turned the lamp and its empty lead petal toward the room's center. Beneath the lamp, laid out in a grid on a small table, was a collection of skeleton keys, many rusted, and some so corroded they would crumble if handled roughly. From where she sat, the collection looked like a chess board, some contemporary, stylized version, at first rather interesting, amusing—and then nothing, so what?: keys in a pattern of columns and rows. She looked back to the dressing table and pulled a hatpin from a tall holder painted with forget-me-not and lilac. The shrill sound of metal drawn across china disheartened her as though this sound with its high pitch were the sound of doubt.

"Lisa, what's taking you so long? Come on."

"I can't decide, come help me," she shouted. When she heard the creak of her mother starting down the hall, she shouted again, "I'm not sure I want to wear this. I made it too fancy, didn't I?" Elisabeth came around the doorjamb dressed in a long white dress with lace furbelows. She held a broad, plumed hat at her side, its crown stuck with a hatpin studded with marcasite and amethyst.

"Sweetheart, even people who know how to sew don't create dresses like the one you made just by the seat of your pants. Now come on, don't spoil this."

"I made it from pictures. Who cares. Anybody can copy a picture."

"What picture? Show me."

"Why did I choose black? It's like I'm in mourning, like Mrs. Danvers in *Rebecca*. Why'd I do that?"

"Because black is elegant and because this is supposed to be a fancy-dress ball. Now, what is it? You want to stick one of these down your hair? I'm not sure that will work. Why don't I put a brooch through the bow of your hair ribbon?"

"I look too much like a little girl, a little girl dressed in black. Great. Maybe, maybe I should put my hair up? Shouldn't I?"

"You should do what you're going to do. Just hurry, we're late."

"Can I sit here at your table?"

"Well, you're there—what's to stop you now? Come on."

She started up from the bench and moved out the door toward the bathroom for her brush and some hairpins. "Mom, what if we're the only ones dressed up?"

"Since it is a dress ball, I sincerely doubt that will—"

"But it's the first year and maybe people won't do it."

"Jesus God, Lisa, come on."

SHE COULD FEEL THE SWIRL of hair atop her head move gently as she and Elisabeth walked down East Spain Street through the light from streetlamps and front porches. She could hear a band playing in the plaza and this sounded a bass accompaniment to the sweet light melody of the jet beads tapping against one another and to the gentle consonant syncopation of the taffeta and silk of their dresses rustling against the cool night air. They walked single file under the balcony of the Blue Wing Inn, their steps slowing on the uneven cobbles, and then came abreast again along the stone wall of Vella's Creamery, which stood across the street from the plaza. They could see the courthouse at the plaza's center draped with small white lights, and as they neared the lawn and parking lot which had been cordoned off as the ball's official area, they heard the deep, sibilant sound of many people talking at once.

"You see. You had nothing to be afraid of. Everybody has made total fools of themselves and dressed pretty much the way you have."

"Very funny." She turned her head down to look at her

waist, her fingers moving to the cummerbund to smooth the satin fold. "Do you have our tickets?"

"Don't lose anything from that dress tonight," Elisabeth said. She reached into a silver-mail purse which hung on a thin chain at her wrist. Lisa watched her pull two tickets from the purse's dark opening, snap the two balled prongs closed with a click, and then raise her hand gently, making the chain slide down her arm toward her elbow, the purse fluttering at her waist and bodice like a bird's wings against a white curtain.

She strayed from her mother's side, her dress rustling past other long dresses or brushing over the tops of men's boots. Occasionally she saw someone she went to school with or who knew her mother. In these instances she would look down as though she hadn't seen them and then change the direction of her wandering; she felt proud of her dress and then over-elegant for the occasion, ostentatious and silly. She wanted to be alone in a sunny room of parquet floors with lozenges of light paving a crystal path above the hard wood, a path she could see through, see down into, and yet a path which kept her suspended, breathing easily, but moving forward, beyond. Beyond, she thought, beyond. A drum solo tattooed evenly into her thoughts and then a smashing of crystal; the clear path broke beneath her and she stood feeling the hemp cordon in her hands and the seething pressure of hundreds of people moving about her.

Two men passed her, wearing high boots, the polished shins of leather reaching almost to their knees. Their steps sounded heavy, dead against the asphalt, but the thickness of this sound pleased her and felt edgeless and unshrill. All around her she heard quick-witted, animated speech.

She watched the feminine curve that distant lights gave to people's faces and thought, just for a moment, that she could see the salience spark in the pupils of their eyes. She felt a particular interest in the light of women's eyes on clear, truce-like nights away from considerations. Why were they so rarely like this? Why were they so much more often cloaked and furtive? She assumed that people needed romance and elevation and exhilaration in their lives. She could not understand why they lived so resignedly the other way. Why did they tolerate the beige day-to-day so willingly? Wasn't love boundless in the rustle of silk, in the feminine curve that candlelight gave to everything, in the ease that laughter lent to women?

She moved through groups of people talking, neared people dancing, their costumes flopping crazily to the sound of the band. She saw a girl and a boy from school throw themselves against this beat as though it were a body of black water they must make their way through. She watched for a moment and then turned and started back along the cordon, drawing closer to where she had left her mother. In the music she could not hear the jet beads tapping on her dress, or the soft pad of her shoes.

A white-haired woman stopped Lisa by placing her hand on her shoulder. "Let me see this dress, dear," she said, pushing her gently to turn around, and then fingering the beaded bodice. A small terror rose in Lisa that the woman would touch the beads which lay across her breasts, but she lifted her hands and then once again moved Lisa to turn and stop so that she could inspect the long bustle of satin gathered and poufed down the dress's back. "Where did you get this dress? It's absolutely sumptuous," the woman said, pulling at her waist to bring her around to face her again. "I don't think I've ever seen anything like it."

"I made it." She spoke quietly, her voice almost soundless beneath the band's percussion. "I made it up."

The woman smiled quickly, the movement brushing across her face the way a cloud can pull a brief shadow across a field. "No one just makes up a dress like this, dear."

As the woman moved away she brushed her hand across

Lisa's cheek. Lisa smelled the scent of gardenia and of cigarettes; she turned to watch the woman in her morning dress
of blue-and-white-striped cotton. The woman held a parasol
with a mother-of-pearl handle and stepped with anticipation,
as though the evening—her way through the evening—was lit
with promise. Lisa thought of the night she had fashioned the
bustle on her skirt—the skirt clothespinned on a hanger
hooked around the doorknob of her closet door, a candle
burning on her dressing table, the black satin burnished by
the yellow light, her eyes intent on how the light played on
this pouf or that, gauging to make sure of the dress's effect in
the night, her hands stitching underneath the satin, here and
there, pulling out a stitch and replacing it, draping the fabric
more fully here, more tightly there, until the effect was as she
had seen in a *Godey's Lady's Book* from the 1850s. She had
then strung yards of tiny jet beads. She worked the needle
through hundreds of their minuscule holes until a long strand
of beads, like oiled black seeds, hung before her and she
draped the string down and around, festooning each crest of
the satin bustle.

She watched until the woman's white dress folded into the
night and the dark throngs of people. She thought of what
the woman had said and felt ashamed, as though she had
caught her in a lie; she had seen pictures, this was true, though
no one had shown her how to construct the dress, nor the
bustle—these she had just done, black-threaded needle in
hand, an image, an effect held in her mind, guiding her, the
yellow candlelight rippling the water of the moiré and the oil
of the satin and the beads.

She looked up to see her mother in a group of people. She
could not hear Elisabeth's laughter but recognized instead the
gestures of her laugh: the blond head thrown back and then
quickly pulled forward into the left hand where it rested a
moment moving back and forth before she lifted it again to

the conversation. Mrs. Armstrong stood there alongside David
and the Andersons, who ran the electrical shop just off the
plaza. The music stopped and Lisa heard their laughter across
the dim asphalt. She watched David raise his arm to smooth
back the straight blond hair from his face, his hand coming
back behind and down his head to gather the hair that feathered at his collar into a tail. It was his gesture, she thought;
she had seen him do it a hundred times at the house, dinner
finished, the plates cleared, the table left with wineglasses,
and she whisked upstairs to bed, where she would lie very
still listening to their voices ebb and flow beneath her like an
underground spring, this trill and murmur smoothing her,
spreading her almost into sleep until their stockinged feet made
the old bitter witch in the staircase groan and cackle, and then
she was wide awake, every sound they made loud in her ears,
too loud and somehow unappeasable, not the sound of their
voices, but the sounds which came from under their voices
or over, sounds not of speech but of something else deep and
sorrowful and desperate, the sounds of the caged half-human
animal in a Sherlock Holmes story or one by Edgar Allan Poe.
She never knew how to think about what she heard on those
nights. In her mind she saw the candles fluttering, the wine
motionless in the bowls of the wineglasses, the dinner dishes
scattered about the kitchen sink and counters like the still,
unhappy faces of clowns. She saw the quick, warm dart of her
mother's eyes and that same quick motion in David's; she
knew that high quiver in her gut just before they sent her
upstairs to bed. But then there were the sounds of the later
night, sounds which made her wonder what she would see
were she to tiptoe down the hall and look in on them in the
room with the shades that glowed like pearls from the street-
lamp below. Would she see her mother and her lover stretched
alongside each other like two tree roots just below the ground?
Or would they be transformed, twisted and furred, hunched

within a cave, their language muted, physical, bald, the sound of something huge and enginelike laboring? She felt confused yet she could not think of the confusion. Her mind saw the red wine motionless in the glasses, the light catching the glass from behind, the fingerprints delicate as spiderwebs on the clear surface, delicate as lace on a pane of glass.

She wondered if David and her mother would begin to see each other again. He had left for Saudi Arabia two years earlier, in the fall, to build a palace out of a grained red stone from India, slabs of which he had leaned up against the doorjambs and table legs in his house. She watched him pour glasses of water down their streaked surfaces to ascertain how the grain would lighten or darken, a towel beneath them catching the play rain, the water from the kitchen faucet. He took the slabs outdoors into the sun and watched them dry, and indeed, they dried in a pattern, the water working down along the dark tributary lines of the stone. Different evaporation rates; fuck, he had said, and then remembered she stood behind him. He grimaced slightly, said something about cement and slumps which, because of the "fuck," she did not ask about and then they walked back into the house, into the living room, where the blueprint unrolled on the floor was as large as a bathroom. He pulled a book from a stack on the floor and showed her a picture of the Saudi terrain, of the unrelenting white sand, and up out of this undulating sheet she imagined the palace he had designed and would build. And then he had gone away, his little house near the olive grove closed up, her mother hardly mentioning his absence or his name or whether he meant anything to her or not, his presence fading, being sanded over by a windstorm, the Rub' al Khali desert absorbing him.

He looked to Lisa the way he had always looked: tall, his thinness taut, compact. She supposed he was tan, though, or somehow changed by the desert as Lawrence of Arabia had been changed. He wore a coat with tails whose corners were folded inward and joined with large brass buttons. Occasionally he moved his hand to Elisabeth's waist. But Lisa noticed he never left it there for long, the hand lifted away, hovering a moment behind Elisabeth's back, indecisive, the action so unlike David's usual calm sure sense. She felt a dull exhaustion, as though his hesitation, his pause at what had once been supple and elegant and right, were somehow her fault—her rejection of him tacit within her mother's. She breathed deeply as though full lungs could throw off this weight.

The band started to play a slow song and David and her mother started from the group toward the dance area. Lisa moved quickly back along the rope; she watched her mother bow gently into the hollow of David's body, the broad plumed hat her mother held covering his back, her dress flowing about his legs like foamy surf, the music plaintive, feeble, the night about them like a great black shell. She wanted her father to be there, holding her, his body reaching above hers like a fine bough, his eyes peaceful, happy, the eyes of a father, she thought, quiet, without suggestion. She turned and walked to the ticket taker dressed as an Indian and asked him to stamp her hand for reentry. She slid past his leather and beads and the groups of costumed people waiting to get in.

She walked through the black-barked elms in the direction of the street and the lighted shop windows along the plaza. She wanted to walk the square and window-shop, *lécher les vitrines*, her mother called it, lick the windows, a phrase Elisabeth had learned back East from a Frenchman who had taught her music theory, *"lécher les vitrines*—rumination upon things one cannot have," her mother had said sternly, her cheeks faltering gently and then pushing back into amusement and then laughter, "things one cannot have, things one cannot have," counterpoint in Lisa's ear with her mother's cool beautiful laughter.

In the jewelry store window a collection of old watches lay among celluloid collars, leather collar boxes, shirt studs, and a stuffed ferret raising his long neck to peer into the luffing wings of a stunned pheasant. She liked how the ferret's eyes matched the set of ruby studs which sat like drops of blood on the stiffly starched plastron of a man's dress shirt. Her eyes moved to the pocket watches, which seemed to her bulky and heavy, jowl-like even, and then on to a gold matrix watch fob which lay circling a bloodstone intaglio set into a huge gold ring. She had seen the fobs and the watches before; they were reminding her of some time long ago, a bad time, she thought, a time she did not want to remember but was remembering in some impressionistic way, a time she was ashamed of, and then the exact image was in her mind of the pictures on the wall of the courthouse cafeteria, the pictures of the early settlers of California with their sturdy wool vests and their heavy fobs swooping across their chests. She moved her eyes to the blue and russet of the pheasant feathers; the music seemed a weak pulse through the elms of the plaza; she wanted to push the past away just as she could push a book back behind other books on a shelf where it would become forgotten by everything but the dust.

She walked on to the black-and-white marble entry of Lynch's Pharmacy. Above her stretched a frosted-glass transom with a Rexall symbol. She looked through the door past the marble soda fountain with wire-back stools to a platform where on some days a shoeshine man wedged playing cards down the sides of the men's shoes he polished so that nothing got on their socks. She and her father had had lime Cokes there one afternoon and the little stooped man had drawn cards, two knights and a queen and an ace of spades, and then, cupping the cards in the palms of his smudged hands, had rounded them down into Neville's shoes almost as if he were forming a pot on a potter's wheel, and the cards had appeared on either side of her father's ankles, the courtly faces peering without expression, the ace somber and colorless.

Now, no one was in the pharmacy, and the lights seemed too bright, derogatory even. She thought about going to see her father tomorrow, about staying in her old bedroom, the bed he had bought her, the only piece of furniture in the room, the hollow brass headboard thumping once against the wall every time she got in bed, a sound like the tumbler of a lock, the room's emptiness surrounding her, mocking her.

"Lisa," she heard someone say behind her. She turned slowly. She didn't really want to see anyone she knew, or to have to talk. He was tall and broad, brilliant at math, and a varsity basketball player, the combination always attractive to her, though she had remained shy of him, his solid hugeness stopping her in the hall, his face intent on her, the hazel eyes quiet, full of questions, and her fumbled excuses as she sidled past, praying she didn't trip as he watched, praying he wouldn't come after her and corner her as his body always seemed to do no matter how or where it stood.

"Hi, Bill. How are you?" She could see that he had left Ron Wilson and Alana Adams on the corner. They watched for a moment, their faces curious, bemused, and then turned away.

"I'm fine," he answered quickly, his own questions more imperative. "What are you doing walking around alone?" He raised his hand to rest against the door header. She felt enveloped by him.

"I'm just"—she paused—"looking at the windows. I like"—she hesitated again—"looking at old things."

"Are you coming to the games this year? You came once last year. Once."

"How do you know that? You're supposed to be playing, not counting." She wasn't being coy with him. She felt flattered but sheepish, embarrassed, as if the moments she spent with him were one long flinch. "I don't really have—"

"I'll pick you up, you know that. Anytime." He leaned in closer to her, the light showing the gold in his pale brown hair. He wasn't being aggressive or angry; he wanted very earnestly to know her and she could feel this and it made it worse, this guilelessness. She could hurt him.

"What I was going to say was that I don't really understand the game of basketball. I don't follow it very well. It's wasted on me."

"I'll teach you—"

"You'll be on the court—" Her words flew at him sharply, too sharply, much more so than she meant. He dropped his arm from the header and looked out toward the street. Cars cruised the plaza.

"What kind of old things?"

"What?" she said.

"You said you liked looking at old things. Like what? Like this?" He gestured at the pharmacy windows, the collection of pharmaceutical implements, mortars and pestles, pewter tablet molds and calibrated vials.

"Yes, like this."

His eyes rested on her. "I had an uncle who was a pharmacist. He killed a little boy. Accidentally filled a prescription with penicillin—kid was allergic to it."

"And he committed suicide," she said, knowing instinctively what the past tense had meant, knowing without thinking about it. "An overdose."

"An overdose. Every possible drug lined up right there in front of him." He paused and gazed down the narrow length of the pharmacy as though he could see his uncle standing behind the high white counter. "And then to make sure, to make sure they didn't find him and save him, he swallowed a bullet too. Old things. That's what old things mean to me." His voice hoarsened. "Anyway, the offer stands."

She watched him walk away, his gait quickening to catch his friends. Then she continued down the street. She moved slowly from storefront to storefront. She hadn't wanted to make him angry, hadn't wanted to make him remember a bad memory. In the fabric shop window were costumes from the 1900s on wire mannequins, and at the hardware store, the display was of the Mother Lode and everything a prospector could need in the mountains: picks, coarse rope, iron skillets, flumes and shallow pans for sifting. She crossed at the corner and passed General Vallejo's barracks, the cheese factory, and the Greyhound bus depot, the lithe blue dog on the sign almost completely obscured by wisteria canes. Across another corner stood the Sonoma Hotel, and in the streetlamps she thought the building's pointed Victorian gingerbread hung like huge grayish stalactites. Parked just outside the hotel's bar entrance were five motorcycles, their front wheels extended before them by long tubes of chrome. She decided the whole scene was icy, the grayish building, the chrome, the hard bellows of laughter from inside the bar. She moved on, her dress brushing down the curb, the smell of the sewer wafting up to her. She passed the florist's window filled with baskets and straw hats, wooden pitchforks and hoes with handles as polished as a fine Georgian chair she had once seen in an antique shop. She looked into the cookshop windows set with spongeware and milk-glass pieces and read a placard about itinerant glassworkers who came to each farm or vineyard and sat before a washbasin of milk blowing the molten sand into shapes which they revolved slowly in the milk, turning the transparent surfaces cloudy and then white.

Before the Assay Office window, which was now the Chamber of Commerce window, she silently repeated her mother's definition of *lécher les vitrines*, the rumination upon things one cannot have, cannot have, cannot have. These words kept pushing in on her and she realized that the window before her contained legal documents, deeds of trust, land grants made by the Spanish government and the Mexican Republic and even by Russia, and that this window was yet another window filled with history, filled with the past, the actual facts of an evolution, a frontier settled. This history was history framed by glaziers and lighted by electricians but it was not something which she could not have, not something which she could deny, and before her the foxed documents reminded her of what she could not undo, could not "not have." Bill was right about old things; and he was wrong.

At the curb she waited for cars to stop and then crossed the street to the plaza. She passed under the dark elms and through the deserted playground, past the sandbox, its surface dug full of holes, choppy as an ocean, and then past the canted seesaw and the slide like a silvery-blue tusk in the streetlight. She walked around the courthouse and toward the Indian, who said when she showed him her stamped hand, "Hey, there's quite a bit of wampum on that dress." It took her a minute to get what he meant, and so she had to turn back to him and laugh. He winked at her, the straight feather in his headband nodding ever so briefly.

"Have you been dancing?" her mother asked. She tried to stay back, tried to make her mother turn from the group so that the conversation wouldn't suddenly be focused on her. She felt shy of David, his two-year absence like a dark room between them, and of David's mother, though she had spoken with her easily enough at the bakery. There was something about the way David and his mother usually seemed to know they belonged where they were, and without question, the world there for their choosing, their maneuvering, their deeming. She admired this assurance, this ease, marveled at it as though it were unbelievable, unattainable. But she had seen David waver, and this saddened her. Her mother walked with her a few paces.

"I'll meet you at home," she said. "There's a pin sticking me and I can't find it."

"Have you said hello to David?" her mother asked, the plume of the hat she held moving like white smoke in the night air. "He's back from Saudi."

"I know."

"Well, then you should say hello, welcome him back." But instead she thought of the awkwardness of seeing her father after the long months away from him, always the rigid silences, the simple verbal exchanges overgrown and choked with meaning. David was here, waiting to be said hello to, but the duty of this politeness coupled with the anxiety of spending the next days with her father seemed overwhelming, consuming, a creature with hundreds of hands pressing her into herself, her cheeks and forehead into her skull, her shoulders and back into her spine, her stomach into her throat.

"I'll be back. Then I'll say hello. Okay? It will just take a few minutes."

"What's wrong, sweetheart?" Elisabeth walked with her for a few more steps. She heard the amber tone come into her mother's voice, the soothing, honeyed modulation as though her mother could lift her from the world she was in, as though her voice could be a great balmy cloud which would buoy her like a puffball and float her to a world of vigor and obscurity.

"Nothing's wrong, Mom. Honest. Nothing at all. I'll be right back."

She began to move away. An electric guitar riff hovered in the night air. "God, this is banal music," her mother said. Lisa stopped and listened for a moment, the sound like bedsprings screeching, amplified. No, she didn't like it, but then, it wasn't asking to be liked, she thought, it wasn't charming or beautiful or profound, it wasn't even particularly interesting, no, it was more like listening to a bird caw, that anguished soul deep in the feathered gut, its desperation frozen on one sound repeated over and over.

"It's not that bad," she said. "You shouldn't really listen to it."

"How the hell does one not 'listen' to music?" her mother asked, her voice calm, amused, her head tilted down, her eyes wide, waiting. Lisa heard the high-pitched cry begin to falter and then the whole band came in and the night surged with sound. She shouted words to her mother which were words only in that she formed them with her mouth and tongue and breath. Nothing could be heard above the band, it was like a violent storm surrounding her, her speech weltering in her throat, the world physical, massive, inarticulate, and she at the eye where no one could reach her, and from where she could reach no one.

She would drive across a country someday, a long barren terrain, the insect whir of the car like a veil of sound which would soundproof her from all other sound. Then she would rest, she thought, her words in the hermetic car meaningful only to her, damaging only to her, retractable as they had not been before.

The music subsided and David stood next to her. She recognized his smile as forced through some type of puzzlement.

"I'm taking this kid for a spin," he said to her mother. "Someone needs to teach her how to dance. Finally." His hand pushed gently at the small of her back, the fingers spread there as though he were spanning an octave on the piano. He pressed her toward the dancers, who now stood quietly waiting for a new song to begin. She felt great relief from his hand at her back moving her, guiding her, taking for a moment all the vast weight of decisions and directions. If only she could work her way up into his body along the slender column of his chest and lie there like a long smooth muscle, deep and safe.

"Do we have to dance?" she asked, the voice of the bass guitarist rasping "Thank you" over the microphone.

"You always have to dance, you know that," he said, his hand still impelling her gently.

"You know what I mean." She stopped and spun her back around away from his hand.

"You weren't going to say hello to me, were you? You're mad at me. I'm almost flattered. I don't think anyone's ever cared whether I came or went."

"I'm not mad at you. I was going home."

"You're at a ball; you can't just go home. Where's your sense of romance?" He took her elbow and led her away from the dancers and the band and in the opposite direction of where his mother and her mother stood. "A lot goes down in two years."

"More like a lot comes up," she said. She could feel his fingers pressed tightly into the crook of her elbow. She didn't know what she meant; she tried to bring the conversation back to the surface: "I'm sure your mother missed you. My mother missed you."

"Your mother did not miss me."

"How do you know that?" she asked. But she knew he was right, her mother hadn't missed him, or hadn't seemed to, the days calm and smooth after his departure as though he had been merely a finger dipped gently into the pool of Elisabeth's life, and as softly withdrawn.

"You should know your beautiful mother better than that," he said, and dropped his hand away from her elbow. He looked over the heads of people who stood near them and then turned his head down to her, his look appraising, almost cold with intensity.

"What should I know?" It was a serious question, one she wanted an answer to. There was something in her mother that she could not fathom, could barely recognize in any systematic form. It seemed like a rigid desire for something Elisabeth never spoke of, never revealed, an old lover perhaps, or the

idea of that lover; or an impetus which directed her, channeled
her, impelled her though she did not always seem aware of it
pushing her, guiding her. She turned to look across the throng
of people. She could barely see her mother's blond hair swept
up and twisted against her tall neck. She was lovely, not
beautiful, no, it wasn't beautiful, that wasn't the word, Lisa
thought. Her mother was lovely, that word having the degree
of delight in it that she saw people take in Elisabeth's features,
her laughter and ease. Lisa knew that at home it was now she
who reached her hand to the back of her mother's head; it
was no longer her father's heavily veined hand, nor David's
touching lightly there and holding with that moment of possession which was not possession but delight. Beautiful implied a necessary distance, like a docent speaking in a
museum—beautiful—a word that had taken time and obser-
vation and cold respect to utter, to know. She knew "beautiful"
was not the word her mother could withstand, could live into
old age being. She recalled the party her father had given her
mother for her thirtieth birthday, recalled being five years old
and helping to dim the lights and clean the long-stemmed
glasses and then standing quietly in the entry-hall closet listening to the murmur of voices, like the murmur she stood
within now at the ball, that sibilance, that ocean of words that
became waves, currents, tides, eddies, that ocean playing upon
the shores of her mother's solitude sensuously, winning her
almost to this definition by others. But she knew how anxious
her mother was about others' perceptions of her, how sooner
or later Elisabeth fought the wooing sibilance and insisted on
the hard sense of her existence as a woman with something
that would fade and slowly rumple from the gravity which
pulled at her like rain-drenched clothing. It had been the
morning after the birthday party, and she overheard the conversation from her bedroom. Her door was open and the living
room had not yet been carpeted. Words came across the boards

as though her parents were skipping stones to her bed, flat, round, perfectly explicit stones which skipped one last time onto her bed and into her ears, where they stopped one after the other like a path pointed out. She had walked from stone to stone, knowing them to be perfect, understandable, neat words which somehow did not register their meaning in her mind for several years.

"It's tiring," she heard her mother say.

"Treat it like a cross, it will be a cross," her father said.

"It is a cross. I don't want this, I never asked for it, I hate the responsibility."

"What responsibility?"

"I don't have the fucking generosity to look like this. This, this should be a gift you give to people, something you allow them to enjoy. I hate it, I hate having it, having to live up to it. I remember when I was eighteen and a candy striper and all the old people just loved having me come into their rooms, me, because I had this and they loved looking at this and I hated them because this was all of me they wanted."

David cupped his hands around Lisa's shoulders and turned her to face him. "Where are you?" he asked.

"Here," she said, laughing. "I'm right here."

"No. You were somewhere far away."

"Thinking about knowing my mother," she said.

"I missed you."

"I wasn't thinking about it that long."

"I missed you while I was in Saudi." The music began again, the sound this time softer, more lyrical, an acoustic guitar replacing the electric, and a woman with long black hair singing.

"Did you miss my mother?" she asked.

"Yes, but that doesn't seem to have mattered—"

"No, you're wrong. She just wants to be missed for the right reasons."

"Reasons known only to her."

"I don't know—I mean, I do know—but it's hard to talk about." The singer pushed her hair back behind her shoulders and stood in profile. Lisa watched her hold the microphone in both hands as though praying, the dim lighting an aura around her, her hair flowing smoothly down her back like a veil. "Look, an apparition," she said.

"Your mother?" He had turned and was looking back to where Elisabeth stood with his own mother.

"No, the singer. She looks like the Virgin Mary."

"Oh."

"I don't miss people as a rule," she said. "I mean, either they're there or they're not."

"That's convenient." He was looking down at her again.

"But they're probably off doing something better, more interesting, and that's good. Why resent that?"

"It means you're letting yourself off the hook—or not permitting yourself to be on the hook. Similar to your mother, except you're doing it before you even know why. You're just taking her word for it."

"Why shouldn't I? She's my mother," but she didn't even know what he was talking about. She felt some urgency to answer his questions, or to foil them. She wanted him to go on talking to her, she wanted him to tell her things, but at the same time she didn't want him to either. It was as though the wrong person spoke to her, someone who shouldn't know anything about her but who did and was wagging it in front of her, and it was fascinating and squalid all at once.

"Come on. I'm supposed to be dancing with you," he said, drawing her toward the platform of musicians.

"You're angry, aren't you?" She felt his hand at her waist, his thumb through the taffeta pressing her rib cage. "I'm sorry you missed my mother and she didn't miss you."

"Don't you two ever talk to each other?" he asked. "Elisabeth was delighted I left for Saudi, absolutely delighted, and you don't even know why, do you?"

"I'm sure she wasn't delighted."

"I made the mistake one day of complimenting you. I might as well have taken you to bed."

His hand pushed at her waist. They moved awkwardly, as though a third body were between them, bumping back and forth between their shoes. She felt uncomfortable with what he was telling her, uncomfortable and yet pleased: he had complimented her and she felt warmed by this and then ashamed because David was her mother's friend, her mother's lover.

"I need to go home," she said.

"Your father's coming for you tomorrow, isn't he? And you'll be gone and then you'll come back depressed."

"I don't come back depressed."

"You always do." She heard the roar of motorcycles starting up across the plaza. She envisioned the cold silver chrome of the choppers in front of the hotel. "And it takes several days to get you out of it too." She felt a burning in her bladder and an uneasiness in her stomach. Her kidneys constricted at the base of her back.

"Could you please tell my mother that I've gone home?" She pulled away from him, her hand that he had held aloft in his own cooling in the night air. "I'm glad you're back."

She hurried through the crowd and out through the break in the cordon where the Indian stood. She kept her eyes to the ground till she had passed him. She reached the sidewalk which led from the plaza, and then, slowing, stretching her arm out to trail her fingers across the cat-tongue granite surface of a monument, suddenly tripped against a series of jagged rocks which bordered a flower bed. She felt a dull wrench in her ankle, and as the plaza grew silent between the band's numbers, she tried not to think of her father or of David or of why Castro Valley and the old house depressed her.

She walked past the creamery and under the balcony of the
Blue Wing Inn, the granite's texture still tingling in her fingers
and the slow, steady mount of pain in her ankle. She walked
harder on it as though to press it past the point of pain, as
though it were a kink which could be gotten out. It flashed
in her mind that she had no house key, that her mother had
it tucked in the silver purse which moved like a trapped bird
about her arm. The key business had started soon after the
move from Castro Valley, had started the week she lost a key
playing in the field behind the house, and after the Saturday
her father came for visiting rights and sat in the front room
on furniture which had once been the furniture in his home—
her father talking amiably but looking around him as though
he were seeing things he had never seen before, as though he
were making an inventory of a past he could not quite remember. She knew the key had fallen from her pocket and
now lay rooted in the field somewhere among moist shafts of
wheat. She could see a thin spine of this grass growing up
through the key, the thin spine bowed gently by the breeze
along with the others but anchored by this small brass object
at its base.

The key lay in the field somewhere; she had not given it to
her father. But her mother thought this, believed this, believed
it enough so that she had begun to place a tiny piece of paper—
the slip from a fortune cookie—in the door when she pulled
it shut behind her. And always now, when her mother came
home, she stooped carefully before the door to inspect it, to
make sure the paper was where she had left it before she
unlocked the door, watching the paper's gentle, faltering flight
which seemed to so reassure her that no one had been in the
house. For years now she had watched her mother bend to
inspect the doorjambs; she felt forgotten in these moments,
the door, the fortune paper, her mother and her father, all a
world she stood back from and viewed, a world which con-
trolled hers without making her a part of it. She had lost her

key in the field of wheat which stretched behind the house all the way to the train tracks—she kept saying this to herself as though she must learn that the field was now her home, her world.

She thought again about that first morning when her father had come for visiting rights and about how her mother had not been hospitable, had not offered him anything to drink or asked him to stay for lunch. She felt wearied by the morning, by her parents' bright gloom—she could describe it no other way. They asked questions of each other that did not mean anything, questions about her dentistry and her school and her clothes, questions about money and real estate in Sonoma, empty, obvious questions. She walked down to the plaza with her father to sit at Gino's and order sandwiches and listen to the dice hit the bar with that snap and scatter sound she liked because it was always followed by an exclamation of some kind, either mock anxiety or triumph, the response never grand, never more than something which could not be walked away from. She liked the cool black shade of Gino's, the huge sandwiches she could not get her mouth around, and the waitress who had arms like a man and smiled at her father without restraint. She wanted the waitress to return over and over to the table. She asked for water, for an extra napkin, for another pickle—anything for the waitress to come and smile at her father with that openness that she, Lisa, could not show in front of her mother and then could not show away from her mother because she had watched her father's lawyer across the marble hall tell him that she had not wanted to live with him. She knew as she wrung the paper napkin in her lap that she had never said those words, had never even formed them on her lips, but that they, the judge and the lawyers and her father, had known she had meant those words, or, if not meant them, had made them come true even though she had never articulated them.

A thought could become—she had learned this—a thought could be a predestination, a disease slowly darkening the soul and mind and heart, and that morning, the bright gloom of her parents' exchanges had sounded as though all had come to pass the way they'd expected it would. She thought she was beginning to fathom the "I told you so" tone of her parents, the pessimistic inevitabilities they seemed to accuse each of bringing on the other.

Along the west side of the house the cottonwoods like a line of dark soldiers moved stiffly in the breeze. She stood beneath them in the blackness for a very long time. In the distance she could hear the band from the plaza. She thought of the many hours she had sat on the back stoop waiting for her mother, the cold cement under her bottom, her homework spread about, the sound of passing traffic from in front of the house, the carport standing empty, her ears almost desperate to hear the crunch of the Mercury's tires on the gravel drive. She knew every plant that lined the carport, its particular shade of green, the different leaves, long and narrow and slightly arched like saber blades, or those tiny clustered thumbprint leaves, mouse-ear leaves, and the many different ferns, the wispy float of their fronds in the damp, breezeless air. She knew the back of this house so well, where the paint on the siding cracked and curled, where the paint was smooth as marshmallow, and where a hook screwed in high up the wall cast down two long streamers of rust. She pictured her mother and David at the ball, their acknowledgment of each other almost lazy.

After a while she walked under the eaves of the carport, the gravel sounding beneath her feet. The driver's side of the Mercury was open. She slid behind the steering wheel, careful not to catch the jet beads of her gown, and pulled the door closed. The light went off and the car was dark and smelled the way it never smelled in the daytime, dank and old. She turned the radio on and found a station playing folk songs. She left it on for only two songs because she imagined the battery dying, having to find positive and negative terminals, and the sparks because the charges weren't clearly marked on the plastic terminal caps. She thought to herself that she knew where the jumper cables were in the trunk, that she was prepared should she need to connect these circuits. Already she could feel the currents jolt up her arm.

She remembered she had no key to the trunk, that she need not submerge her hand into the center of the sparks, that she need not get at the jumper cables, that there was no other car to boost the circuit, and that the battery might not even be dead; she was safe.

But she was afraid—a fear which had started one night long ago when she walked home from the Sebastiani Theater, her shoes sounding differently on the different pavings of cobblestone and tile and brick that surfaced the fronts of the grocery store, the lawyers' offices, Gino's restaurant, and then Vella's Creamery. The air had been still and balmy; she hadn't even thought to be anxious. Then she turned the corner up East Spain Street and walked under the old wooden balcony of the Blue Wing Inn to hear the sound of a persistent stream of water, of urine, from a man standing in the last dark doorway of the inn, the luminous particular of white at his middle.

She reached around and locked the car doors. The windows fogged slowly, demurely, she thought, as though getting ready to retreat into the opaqueness of dawn. Their frosting-over closed her inside the car and she could not see out. She knew that all she need do was reach her hand to the glass and wipe it back and forth, but she didn't move her hand to the window. She seized it into a fist and slammed it against the dashboard; all she wanted in the world at this very moment was a small brass key which would fit the back door and allow her the short passage up the stairs and into her bedroom, where deep within her closet she could sit below the hems and shirttails and hear nothing of the world save her own clipped breathing and the groan of the wood floor as she resettled her weight, her feet pressed up against the blue glass water jug, "the fur coat fund—the college fund," the coins layered randomly like leaves on the ground, the coins stopping mid-jug, an inch above her toes.

She thought of the collection of old keys on the table in her mother's room. She traced on the damp windows the ornate loops and curls of the skeleton keys and decided that when she finally got back inside the house she would take one of the old keys and put it on a ribbon to be worn around her neck. She would at least have a key, she thought, even if it didn't open anything. Her wrist stung, and this coupled with the ache in her ankle angered her even more. And what was making her think of jumper cables and car batteries and old, useless keys? Why was she thinking about all these things?

Her breath began to frost over the loops and curls on the windshield. It didn't matter, she said, there were ways inside the house without using a key. She pulled the long chrome door handle and the lock popped up. She stepped gingerly out of the car onto her ankle and, feeling the sting in her wrist again, knew that she was ready. She stood on the stoop, the night smooth and complicitous around her, like two dark wings along the underside of her arms propelling her, urging her as though beneath their balmy down was a fledgling skeleton that could be hers. She drew her right arm back, the tight cup of the taffeta bodice pulling at her shoulder, and then drove the arm forward through the thin pane of glass shattering about her wrist and forearm, the slicing contact raising a bile in her throat as tiny mica shards settled on the shaking, liquefying surface of her arm and hand.

Her fist unfurled before her in the upstairs bathroom streaked with less blood than she would have imagined. She saw her hand beneath the faucet as a paintbrush being rinsed of its thin medium. She looked up into the medicine cabinet mirror, up past the black-beaded bodice she wore, and saw her face spattered with blood and the skin below her eyes beginning to twitch as the nerves in her body constricted and moved into a rigidity much like mortar when it dries and holds tight what once was loose, even liquid.

THE NEXT MORNING she started out of bed, her heels hitting the floor so suddenly that her knees buckled with the impact. She found herself in a squat, facing the teardrop handles of her dresser. The wood around the handles was dry and she felt the inside of her throat as this dry, streaked wood, and then the dream boomed in her mind and she saw the white sink, the kitchen sink downstairs, and her mother holding her by the waist, feeding her hands down into the garbage disposal, her mother's thin fingers reaching across her arms, across the white sink for the switch. She heard the motor begin to grind, but she could not feel pain.

She was astonished at how soft and malleable the bones of her fingers and hands were, astonished because it was as though they were chicken cartilage or the tumid stalks of spring flowers. She could feel her hands being eaten by the blades, becoming lighter. She looked sideways across her mother's face. The expression sat very calmly there: the face of a mother who must hold her child down for a rabies shot or for a vaccination, something the child must have, some pain the child must endure and which the mother bears calmly because she believes there is reason behind the pain.

She heard the percussion of pans from the kitchen and, pulling a robe on, slowly made her way down the stairs, through the sunlight blazing from the front door. There was the smell of eggs in the air, that sweet, sensual smell, and

David leaning up against the counter, talking, while her mother stood at the kitchen sink in one of his shirts pulling the furred skin off a kiwi fruit with a paring knife.

"What'd we do for green in fruit salads before kiwi came along?" her mother said, turning her head toward her as she came into the kitchen.

"Grapes." She felt a sharp draft from the porch into the kitchen.

"Good morning," David said, his voice carefully soft, his eyes on her hand—her real hand—which she had forgotten until that moment. "Come here, let's see this."

He pressed her down into one of the iron chairs on the back porch, and then squatting, his long legs becoming haunches at either side of her, quietly apologized for not bringing her mother back the night before.

She looked past him to the back door and saw the ell of paper her mother wedged in the door sitting like a white blossom on the linoleum. She wondered how the glass had been swept clean of the floor without the cookie fortune being brushed along with it, and then she haltingly realized the broken door pane would never be mentioned, nor how her hand had come to be this way, nor the evening, because guiltily they thought she had spent the greater part of the night outside, in the dark, waiting for Elisabeth and the house key to come home.

She felt David's fingers moving along the cuts on her hand, trying to gauge how deep they were, whether they needed stitches or not, whether she would be scarred, and then he was holding her foot, turning it from side to side, pressing the feverish green swelling.

"How'd this happen?" he asked, lowering her foot gently to the floor, a sense of relief in his face and voice that he had so quickly found something to talk of other than the hand and the broken pane and last night. She felt like laughing crazily, laughing as a madwoman would laugh, her head thrown back, the teeth bared, the shrill cynicism like a careering car in the midst of order and decorum. No, they weren't going to talk about her not having a house key, or about the fact that she had spent the night alone in a house with the back door as good as wide open. No, they weren't even going to mention it.

She saw that the table was set for three and that a rose floated in a bowl at the center of the table; the bowl's water sat as still as glass under the coral petals. She thought that if she were to look at herself in the mirror of the bowl's water her skin would appear as gray as old meat, and muscleless, the face of an old woman resigned to the briefness of her future. She looked up to see David's smile, grotesque and clownlike, and then she thought of a time many years ago, of tents and animals and that feigned excitement in the air that was really lasciviousness, or so it seemed to her now as she thought of the circus she and her father had gone to in Modesto that year her mother had been away so much playing summer stock and civic light opera. She saw herself and her father walking into the huge green-and-blue-striped tent and recalled how the smell of the dirt and sawdust floor had risen to her nose as though she had pointed her face down between the cardboard flaps of a cereal box. She had held the tickets in her hand, the tickets with the tiger's mouth drawn wide, roaring, in neat lines of type, dates and prices and seat assignments. She held her father's hand with the hand that did not hold the tickets and pulled him up the bleachers, the groan and sway of that scaffolding exciting her, moving her to rise faster and faster up the wooden-plank stairs with her father a gentle solid pull on her momentum under the hot lights as the calliope began its lewd clamorousness against the huge deep sound of the crowd.

They found their seats between an older couple with a young

girl in a pink dress and a family with two little boys who sat so quietly she wondered if they were enjoying the bears who danced with the great metal collars before the crowd, as though there could be nothing extraordinary about bears waltzing to Johann Strauss.

"That's about how I look when I waltz," her father said, leaning his dark head down to her ear but keeping his eyes forward. He put his arm down around her small hips, half pulling her across the seat closer to him and half hugging her. She could feel the raised grain of the old, dry wood through her cotton shorts. The tent lights began to dim as the blue and red lamps of the center ring bloomed to reveal the largest man she had ever seen holding a metal bar high above his head. He turned slowly, his massive arms like the sides of a great ship, and then when the audience had quieted and focused themselves completely on him, he commenced to pull his great fists in toward his serious face till the metal rod framed his head like a Gothic arch. She excitedly clapped her cupped palms, which sounded with the flat slap of the tickets she still held. She recrossed her ankles and swung her feet back and forward, kicking the metal brace below the seat three times before her father laid his hand on her knee to stop. The lights came up in the first and third rings and she quickly moved her head from one ring to the next, trying not to miss the shoot-out between the chimpanzees dressed as cowboys and Indians or the white horse with a plume at its blaze cantering about the ring with a woman in a pink tutu standing on its back, the plume moving as the woman moved, up and forward and back, up and forward and back, the plume and the woman a type of surreal mirror.

She moved forward on the bench, watching the tutued woman circling briskly on the horse's back, her arabesque descending rather too shakily but her narrow body rising none-theless confidently into a handstand before she swung her legs down to the side of the horse, holding the saddle's pommel with one hand and then fisting up her body till she clung to the horse's withers, slowing him, dropping one leg and then the other, both horse and woman coming to a gliding stop in front of a man dressed in riding boots and jodhpurs who took the bridle and offered his palm to the crowd, bidding them to applaud the act, and she, Lisa, had thought her life was going to be that beautiful fleet horse moving gracefully under her.

A very small car drove up just as the applause died and out sprang seven or eight clowns as though a whole clothes closet were exploding, and then an old hobo clown backed himself into the car and pushed it from the arena, leaving the other clowns to frolic and play paddleball with what looked like a girdle springing back and forth between them, the garters flying this way and that. She looked sideways at her father and concentrated momentarily on the new growth of dark beard coming out on his chin and halfway up his cheeks. She reached out and trailed her index finger across the skin's surface, hearing the tiny rasp, and then retracted her hand to quickly clasp it with the other. He had laughed and turned toward her.

"How about something for the breadbasket? Something nutritious. Cotton candy? Caramel apple?"

"Okay," she said, swinging her feet back and banging them into the metal brace. "Sorry."

"Right. I'll be back," he had said, her chin rising as he rose, her chin following his, looking out toward either aisle to see which one afforded him faster access.

"I'd like cotton candy," she said, feeling the sticky pink wool in her mouth already. He turned and smiled at her, waving his hand.

A roar of applause brought her attention back to three toy poodles skipping back and forth between the backs of two ponies, one circling the ring clockwise and the other circling counterclockwise. After several leaps all three poodles landed on one pony, who halted quickly, sending the dogs sliding into a burlap sack held by a clown who flinched exaggeratedly as the dog trainer, a hefty blond woman, flailed him with a switch. She sat through several more acts before she began to feel that her father had been gone a long time. The older couple with the little girl dressed in pink had left a couple of acts ago and she thought the family with the silent little boys sat as still as people waiting in a doctor's office.

The lights came up in the audience and people began to rattle down the bleachers toward the clowns greeting children as they hopped off the last planks of the scaffolding. She had stood up and searched the moving crowd, the hundreds of heads like a heaving vat of marbles. She could not see her father anywhere. She wondered what to do, whether she should try to find the car or perhaps someone who would know where he was. She started down the bleachers, the rattle and sway now making her nervous and more frightened. A clown with metallic-blue hair grabbed her into his arms and put her down again quickly, the dirt and sawdust powdering across her sandaled feet. She hadn't laughed or flinched or squirmed.

"Could you help me find my father?" But the shredded back pockets of the clown's dungarees now faced her. She closed her eyes and for a moment imagined holding her finger to the raspy bristle of her father's whiskers; they had to be close by, perhaps just on the other side of the massive canvas flaps tied back with heavy ropes, perhaps near the lion's cage, which smelled to her the way urine smelled after you ate asparagus. Her eyes occasionally met someone her own height, but always that child's arm extended up near his or her ear, where the fingers were invisible, grasped within a big adult hand.

Perhaps her father waited just beyond the blue-and-green-striped canvas holding cotton candy, his strong broad face there between the pink spun-sugar clouds, his black hair indistinct against the hot black night. She passed through the roped canvas flaps and could see the long guy wires of the tent dimly lit in the moonlight. She milled through the crowd to the closest wire and stood grasping its torqued sinewy strength. Once her mother and father had forgotten to pick her up from school, had left her standing before the corbiestepped edifice with the stone lions who each had a raised paw as though they were shaking hands like trained dogs. The lady principal had come and stood with her, holding her fingers in her thin blue-veined hand which reminded Lisa of the raw veal her mother pounded out for scaloppine. Mrs. Fischer had stood very straight, talking only often enough to remind Lisa of her presence. She left to telephone the Sandhams and her clear good voice sounded far away when she leaned down to report, "Your mother just forgot the time." Forgot the time, the phrase, what it could mean, seemed to stand there between them on the steps, a careful sentry guarding Lisa from some sense she knew she was not supposed to feel and from which she was to be protected. Mrs. Fischer asked her if she wanted to sit down and they sat on the steps between the polite lions and Mrs. Fischer recited a long poem to her about an old shaky cat named Gus who lived by a theater in London. She heard Mrs. Fischer's voice delivering the lines and could almost feel her cool, smooth hand instead of the twisted cable which pulsed stiffly in her fist now as she spotted her father striding toward the big top. She had called to him, and as he turned toward her she saw the anxiety recede from his face as though the boil were going out of water.

"I'm sorry, baby."

"You forgot my cotton candy."

"So, you weren't worried about me? Didn't think I'd dropped dead of a heart attack?"

"You forgot the time," she said.

"No, I didn't forget the time," he snapped, his hand epau-leting her shoulder and turning her toward the row of wagons and small, peaked tents. "Do you still want cotton candy?" he asked, his voice softening. "I had to make a phone call. Let's have our fortunes read," he went on, and then stopped abruptly and hunkered down to her height, pulling her into him, into the concavity of his now stooped torso. "I hate it when you use your mother's expressions." He was calm then, his eyes looking straight into her, past the confused tears graying her vision of bright booths and wagons.

"Come on." He steered her by the shoulders through co-agulations of people standing before the snake charmers and the fortune tellers and a pink-and-white wagon where a two-headed lamb stood, the pink noses nuzzling the bars, the sound in their throats like a chair with rusty casters.

"When it grows up, will it still have two heads?" she had asked after a time, looking back over her shoulder.

"It will probably die soon. Things like that don't live for long. I don't know why, specifically. Mentally retarded people don't live long either. Survival of the fittest—all that, I suppose."

They ate patty melts in a coffee shop near the circus grounds. Her eyes had traced the geometric daisies on a soffit over the open kitchen, and just as her eyes descended a brown stem to a squarish leaf, a woman joined them at the table, leaning into her father to kiss him lightly on the cheek. He asked if she wanted something and she answered, "Just coffee," before she turned, smiling nervously, to Lisa. Her brown hair fas-cinated Lisa, the short sweeps and crests catching light like a chocolate cake with waves of chocolate frosting.

"Mary; Lisa. Lisa; Mary," and she realized that the tele-phone call during the circus had been to this woman sitting in the booth with them, this woman who drove home with them to Castro Valley, to their house, hers and her parents', the menthol of the eucalyptus trees mingling with the last exhaust of the car as they all three went into the house, Lisa thinking of the calendar in her bedroom with the many pictures of English country cottages and the numbered grid of August with only two squares struck through because there was still almost a month before her mother returned home to Castro Valley.

She had asked for a fire, and as her father built it, kneeling before the andirons, she sat in her small chair watching Mary make scotch and sodas at the wet bar, watching her compact body turning back into the room, holding both tumblers in one palm with her fingers up about them like pale petals. The ice chimed gently against the glasses, the fire crackled, and she knew the telephone would ring an instant before it did, splitting the ease to reveal what it had always been, tenuous and temporary.

"Excuse me," her father said over the rings, which seemed to sound louder and more urgent each time. She watched him walk to her parents' bedroom and close the door solidly behind him. The telephone rang two more times and then in the middle of the third ring it stopped. She could not hear her father's voice in the background, but in the foreground she heard the contact of glass with glass as Mary placed the drinks on the table, smiling as the distant flushing of a toilet told Lisa that her father had not answered the call from her mother that came always just before an eight o'clock performance. She traced the chintz flower on the arm of her chair as he came from the bedroom.

"So. What are you going to drink, kiddo?" She had watched the sad, anxious smile jet across his face and then the broad hand reach down too quickly to the drink on the table. He clicked the base of his glass into the base of Mary's glass and said "Cheers" before he raised the drink to his lips.

"Cheers," she said, her gaze returning to the smooth fabric, the greens and pinks she loved.

"We need a proper toast," Mary said, pushing herself up

from the couch. "What do you like to drink, Lisa?" Her voice sounded stern, disappointed, and Lisa could not raise her eyes from the leaves and the long curling tendrils. She knew that once again she had done something wrong, had not listened carefully enough, had said something insulting or stupid. She blinked through clear gray tears. The tendrils were tiny snakes crawling from her fingers out across the room, their silver scales flashing like dust in the sunlight.

"Juice? Milk? Do you have grenadine, Neville?" Mary asked. "We'll make Lisa a cocktail."

"I'll make it," she said, getting up from her chair. "I can do it. I'm seven."

"No. I'm going to do it," her father said, setting his drink down on the table.

The fire snapped as she placed three coasters around the coffee table. She sensed that it might be rude to pick their drinks up and put them on the square coaster boards with the English hunting scenes. She wished that this woman Mary would stop looking at her and pick up her drink. She had put her father's drink on the coaster and walked to the side table where her mother kept cocktail napkins. The drawer had pulled easily and there had been the six familiar stacks of tiny napkins, the Audubon birds ordered from the Metropolitan Museum of Art, the botanical napkins of fruits and vegetables and flowers, the stack of white ones which her mother had hand-painted with watercolors, spreading the napkin out completely on the kitchen counter and delicately painting just the lower right-hand corner before she refolded these and stacked them in the drawer next to the blue napkins with tall white geese, the stack from which Lisa had pulled three.

David lowered her ankle into a pan of water snapping with ice cubes. "When's your father coming for you?" he asked. The question seemed to hover in her mind as though it were tangible: a stream of words, a flowing banner of skywriting across her mind. He was coming for her, wasn't he?

The timer on the oven began to buzz and she heard the oven door drawn open, the sound as though it came from deep within a parrot's throat.

"Two o'clock."

"What about the ankle?" he asked again, pushing the hair back from his face.

"I just stumbled on some rock in the plaza. It's nothing."

"It's a sprain."

She watched her mother serve eggs and the cinnamon pull-apart she had bought yesterday at the bakery. Her hands were smooth and white. David scooted the pan of ice under the table so that she could keep her foot in it while they ate breakfast. "Hi, baby," her mother said, leaning down to kiss her forehead. "Are you all packed?"

"Sort of."

The eggs seemed particularly hot in her throat; her foot was beginning to feel dead and rubbery; the nerves in her face constricted from the ice water and ached as though someone had hit her across the bridge of her nose.

"I think you should show your father around the festival when he gets here. He'll be in time for the gunslinging," David said.

"She's not going to be very good at walking."

"I'll be fine walking," she said, a defensive stiffness ridging her voice, the aches in her body precious to her in that instant, a measure of distinctness apart from her mother and from her father, from David and from the world; it didn't occur to her that the cuts in her hand were actual physical wounds, centers of pain. They were marks of physical individuality, of physical independence caused by singular action and thus a type of freedom and autonomy which she cherished as the insignia of self-control and self-possession.

"Maybe you should put your foot up, though, until he comes," her mother offered, laying her knife across the top of her plate. "Let's put it above your heart to get the swelling down."

"I want to hear you play at the wedding. And I'm going to," she said, the cinnamon bread spongy under her fork, the texture of the cinnamon granular in her mouth and then not as sweet or flavorful as she had expected. The rose floated motionlessly in the bowl. She thought that she could feel her mother gazing quietly at her lacerated hand.

"How about a sip of this fizz?" David offered, lifting the tall cylindrical glass across the table to her. An arch of lime resting on the glass's lip began to tilt as she took the white drink and then it fell, sliding down the rose bowl, in its wake a milky brushstroke.

"I would say that these are the best I've made in two years."

"You cheated, you lazy bugger."

"You let your mother use that kind of language?"

"You're supposed to shake these by hand," Elisabeth said. "The way they do in New Orleans."

"Elisabeth, there is absolutely no appreciable difference in taste. For Christ's sake. I'm not going to shake a jug for forty-five minutes with a blender sitting on the shelf staring me in the face as though I were a complete fool."

She could hear the loud whir of the blender in her head, and the clink and chink of the ice cubes being pushed up and down by the pulsing blades until they were shaved enough to be taken under by the insistent metal wings which shattered them quickly into individual crystals. She could hear the engine of the blender, its deafening din always objected to by her mother. David and Elisabeth had been making Ramos fizzes and the sound of the blender had penetrated her dream to become the garbage disposal eating her hands fed down into the dark, silver-rimmed hole by her mother. She felt within a haze of sounds and for a moment believed that her hand's cuts were from the dream, from the garbage disposal— from the blender, which was real, and not from the broken door pane swept up like an unworked puzzle and secreted in the trash. Of course, she thought, the broken window's slivers had never dropped like tiny guillotines into the flesh of her hand and wrist. What had happened to her hand had happened in her dream, her own mind had conjured it, she had done this thing to herself, and why should her mother or David talk to her about it, apologize, or even anguish over it, telling her that she would have to pay to replace the glass? Her hand couldn't be talked about because it had all happened in a dream and they couldn't know what was in her dreams if she didn't tell them.

And if they did see that her hand was lacerated, they thought it the result of their not coming home all night—the result of their actions, not hers. Her hand might as well have been chewed up by a garbage disposal, or a blender or the rotary of some monstrous machine, it didn't matter, because they didn't know that her hand's lacerations were merely the result of one latent, hugely desired act of independence. They couldn't apologize for something they didn't know had happened; they could only apologize for what they thought had happened, and for their guilt, which was worthless, which had nothing to do with anything other than themselves.

All this embattled her mind as the smooth cream of the fizz lingered on her lips like a kiss. And then, as she swallowed, she noticed the composure of the morning, of the food on the plates, and it became so obviously inevitable that the broken pane wasn't going to be talked about: they wished it had never happened and so, in a way, it hadn't, because their guilty silence would become the important issue rather than what had informed that silence—she assured herself they knew that old trick.

"SO, WHAT'D YOU DO to your hand?" her father asked, concentrating on getting out of Sonoma, past all the police cordons and the lines of cars and trucks pulling horse trailers or flatbeds with carriages and vintage cars tied down like trinkets on a gift. She couldn't think of an appropriate answer to her father's question.

She was apprehensive about telling him that she did not have a key to the house in Sonoma. He would then ask why, and she would have to either lie or tell him that her mother thought she had given it to him so that he could reclaim some of his possessions. They might then talk of the move from Castro Valley and perhaps even of the divorce, subjects they really had never discussed before, subjects full of shame and misgiving.

She could say she had fallen off a horse into some barbed wire, and that could explain both her ankle and her cut hand; he would ask about the horse, about whether she had a friend who owned horses, about who had taught her to ride and the type of saddle, Western or English, and she only vaguely knew the difference. She could try a bicycle accident, but she was sure this would be mentioned to her mother: Doesn't Lisa have reflectors?—or, Is this town too quaint for bike lanes?—or, The alignment on her tires better be checked before she rides that bicycle again.

"I caught it in the garbage disposal," she said, the words coming out of her mouth like an ejection of ice from a machine.

"You did what! The garbage disposal?"

"I thought I heard a spoon or something clicking against the blades and so I turned it off and put my hand down there to feel around, but the blades hadn't stopped yet and they kind of got me."

"Kind of?"

"It's not that bad."

"Did you see a doctor?"

"It didn't need a doctor, they're just superficial cuts."

"Superficial cuts. Where'd you get that phrase?"

"I don't know, the back of the Vaseline jar or something."

"Great. Look, something like that should be tended to. Have you had a tetanus shot recently?"

The car was dribbling over two sets of railroad tracks and she looked out the windshield at the old wood-frame houses that lined the road ahead.

"Dad. It's fine, I'm fine. Okay? I don't want a dumb tetanus shot."

"Dumb tetanus shot. What the hell are they teaching you up here in Vintage City? Tetanus a little too modern for the ambiance up here?"

"I've had my shots."

"When?"

"I thought you got tetanus from rust anyway."

"Sometimes, sometimes not. You've had a booster, though, right?"

"God, I didn't know you needed shots for Castro Valley; do I need my passport too?"

"Smart-ass," he said without much inflection in his voice. "Little smart-ass."

"Dad, I've had my shots. Okay? How's Mary?"

"Mary's great. She'll be there when we get in. What happened to your ankle? That obviously wasn't caught in the garbage disposal."

"I tripped—on a rock—in the plaza. I wasn't looking, I don't know, I was thinking, something, anyway, it just happened."

"Well, did a doctor see this one?"

"It's a sprain, Dad. I need to keep off it, that's all. You know, sprains are like colds, you leave 'em alone and they go away, you don't leave 'em alone and they go away in the same amount of time."

"Superficial too, I suppose?" he said.

She watched a herd of cows move down the side of a foothill toward a white clapboard dairy, their bloated udders swaying beneath them, looking, she thought, very painful, that same heavy, stretched feeling her breasts had before her period every month. "Whatever," she said to her father, and they rode in silence for a time, the foothills undulating like great lengths of flaxen hair at either side of the road. It felt good to her to ride in a car other than the Mercury, this car's smooth black upholstery smelling of leather and her father, and the puzzlingly companionable smell of horses which came from the corral of a riding stable near the road.

"Baby, you want to tell me what really happened to your hand?" She watched her father push the stick shift forward and the car began to slow and then she watched him pull the stick shift back and the car slowed even further, coming to stop at a junction.

"I broke a window with it," she said. "I put it through a window."

"I know," he said, accelerating the car, his hand gripping the wooden knob of the shift. "That much I know."

"Oh."

She thought that he had come to the front door, and then she remembered she had not been ready and he had walked around the house to the rose garden and into the back field planted with wheat and bordered with sunflowers not yet in bloom.

"I sat and watched your mother's fellow close it over with cardboard and duct tape; I didn't assume the wind had blown it out," he said.

"I got locked out and just got angry, that's all."

"Don't you keep a key outside, hidden somewhere?"

"Yeah, there's a key outside." She paused for a moment, knowing she shouldn't say what she was about to say. "There's a key outside. Somewhere."

"What? You don't know where the key is?"

"No."

"Well, what the fuck good is it then if you don't know where it is?"

"She thought I gave it to you."

"Oh, brilliant. Your mother."

"It's my fault, I lost the key in the first place."

"What do you mean, your fault? It's a crime to lose a goddamned house key? Don't be silly; I must have lost twenty keys while I was growing up."

"I think we had different mothers, though," she said, wanting the anger to subside from his voice. "It just doesn't matter, Dad, okay?"

"No, it is not okay. You have to fucking scar your hand in order to get into your own house; that is not okay."

They passed a car pulled to the side of the road, its hood in billows of steam coming off the engine.

"She's just being careful."

"She's being paranoid, Lisa, that's what she's being. And stop protecting her. You can't even see what she's doing to you."

"She's not doing anything to me; she's my mother."

"That's not great logic," he said, looking across at her. Their eyes met and then she looked away and into a car riding alongside them with a young woman driving, her hair pulled back into a pert tail which lifted up from her head and then fell. They broke horses' tails to get them to lift like that, she thought. It was something she had been told while watching one of the Vintage Festival parades: an old man in overalls had leaned down to her and said, "Sister, you know how they get that tail to stand up like that? They break that sucker." She had never said anything about logic, what did that have to do with anything?

"How's school?" he asked. She could detect the quality in his voice that she had begun to hear a few years ago, a tone of resignation mingled with alertness—a type of bitter antic-

ipation—almost like cynicism, except the tone in his voice
didn't seem to indicate he knew the precise shape of the future
as cynics always did. There was also something in his tone
that allowed her to evade whatever question had been asked,
as though they both knew the question at hand was merely a
verbal shroud for the questions that couldn't, or wouldn't, be
asked.

"I have lunch with my friend Maria every day. We walk
down Broadway to her backyard and sit in this little place
covered with ivy."

"Very academic."

"Sometimes. We study our biology together a lot."

"Do you talk?"

"Of course we talk."

"You talk about boys—young men?"

She could feel his gaze on her. "Sometimes. Not really."
He seemed stumped for a moment, as if he weren't sure of
her answer. "Yeah, Dad, sure. I mean, yes, we talk about
boys." He still seemed a little confused to her, or maybe it
wasn't confusion so much as a very mild form of desperation.
It seemed she wasn't saying the right things, or at least wasn't
saying what he wanted to hear. "Do you mean a specific boy,
Dad? Is that what you mean? Like a boyfriend?"

"A boyfriend. Yes. I don't wish to pry, though." A billboard
for a racetrack loomed over the freeway. Extending up from
the huge rectangle of the sign were the heads of three horses,
and just up from the horses' heads were the goggled jockeys
in their colorful caps. She thought of Bill on the basketball
court, his green jerseys—"his silks"—dark with sweat, his
hair wet and falling down across his intent eyes.

"Maria I guess sort of has a boyfriend."

"Oh, what's he like?" he seemed to ask very quickly.

"What's he like?"

"What's he do for a living?"

"Dad, he's only seventeen years old. He doesn't do anything for a living."

"What's this guy David do for a living, then?"

"He's an architect," she said rather slowly. "I thought we were talking about Maria's boyfriend."

"What about you? Don't you have a boyfriend?" he asked.

The populated Berkeley hills reached up to the left of them, and the setting sun caught brightly in the windows of the houses. She didn't know what to answer her father. Sure, she'd been asked out, she'd even been asked to the Senior Prom, but all of this seemed so awkward to her, so much a part of the high whispering in library period, the fashion magazines hidden and opened within the outsize art books, *Seventeen* covering the wary light of a Rembrandt or the brackish darkness of a Van Gogh. She trusted the books beneath, not the high smiling gloss of photography and machine-stitched satin.

"I don't have a steady boyfriend, if that's what you mean. But I don't want one either."

"You learn that from your mother too?"

He changed his grip on the steering wheel.

She could feel her back stiffening, the kidneys constricting, her stomach sucking in upon itself; she could control her body, and her retreat into it; there neither of her parents could accuse her of being just a puppet, there no one had taught her anything. She said nothing. She thought of her bladder infections, the ones that had started soon after she got to Sonoma. She thought about being excused from classes without question and anytime she wanted because the doctor had written strict instructions to her teachers that she was not to be detained from the lavatory, in fact could not be detained, and she would walk briskly from the chalky rooms down the linoleum halls to the silent, multistalled bathroom full of sharp smells and watch the orange urine wash the bowl, and then lie on the cold, wet floor counting the tiles that reached halfway up the walls like wainscoting and unfold the gold wrappers from the chocolate coins the doctor had handed her after he had handed her mother the tablets which caused the curious orange in the bowl; she would be deliciously silent and alone till the loud clash of bells and shoes and doors yanked her from the floor as though a strong arm had reached down and grabbed her shoulders, hoisting her to her feet.

She had learned after a while how to cause the infections in her bladder, how to make the urine cloud and then turn deep red with blood. She rejected salty food, or food that made her thirsty, and it would take three to four days of not drinking any fluids, and hours of holding off going to the bathroom, and then she was once again in the brown-paneled doctor's office, her mother holding the short clipboard on her lap, filling in Lisa's medical history, the urine specimen in its paper sack sitting on the counter for only a moment before the nurse walked it briskly down the hall to the laboratory, which always came back with the same matter-of-fact report: and then the bathroom was once again her refuge, her unassailable excuse, her unbreachable solitude.

"How do you get off campus? I thought you weren't allowed to leave the grounds."

"That was junior high, Dad."

"Oh," he said, his voice sounding distant. "So, what do you do after school, then? Go back to your friend Maria's? I mean, you obviously don't go home; you don't have a key."

"I do so go home, Dad."

"What the hell for, if you can't get in?"

"It's still my house."

She hated that her voice sounded so harsh. But the house on East Spain Street was her house: it wasn't the asphalt grounds screaming with bells, or the long stretches of linoleum patterned as though after petri dishes of mold; it wasn't the high stench of disinfectant pervasive as a quarantine; and sitting on the back stoop doing her homework wasn't that vision of enforced surrender she saw in every slam of a metal book locker, in every sound of the metal crashing into itself, and in its frozen shudder.

"I sit in the back and do my homework. Sometimes I walk through the field to the water tank. There's a little barn back there. I have a little place set up where I can read. It's sort of a desk and chair I made with apple crates. And I have an old jar with sprigs of leaves in it."

"You're almost sixteen years old and you still have a fort? Come on, baby, you can't be serious. That can't be right."

She liked the mottled shade the wispy birch tree shed in Maria's backyard, and the iron rose arch, its rust almost as beautiful a color as the roses it supported; but she liked even better the dusty solitude of the old barn, its breezy creakings sounding all the world to her like the sound of grace.

She had done many a page of homework in that old barn. She thought of an assignment she wrote once on water pollution, using only images as her argument: the surface of a pond orange with dead carp; sea gulls in straitjackets of oil and tar, flightless and wandering like mental patients along the darkened sand; a child wading in red boots, the rubber beginning to smoke and seethe at his ankles, chemically reacting with the water, his hand pinching his nose against the stench. The teacher had flunked her, saying there was no point, no presentation of conflict or argument. Her face burned even now thinking of the paper passed back last because the teacher always arranged them from best to failing, and of the mark slashed across her paper which looked very much like the red gashes across her hand now.

"Dad?"

"Yes?"

"Why don't you and Mary get married?" They passed a truck pulling a boat named *Champagne*.

"Mary and I are fine the way we are. Anyway, we're talking about your fort."

"Don't you want to?" A man was driving the truck with a dog on his lap. "You've been together for a long time."

"Yes. We have."

"Well, I don't know, shouldn't you get married or something?"

"Or something." In the side mirror she could see the head of the dog grow smaller and smaller and then the truck with its boat disappeared from the mirror altogether. On the hills under the live oak trees were patches of shadow, and just ahead was a man pulling long strips of poster off a billboard.

"Did your mother really think I'd try to come into the house and take things?" His voice seemed very even, an evenness that was too even, and too quiet. "Of course, maybe I would have if you hadn't been there."

She wanted to comment on what he had just said, yet she knew that any comment, any response, would open the subject up to a life she was not sure she wished to grant it. She traced the deeply embedded stitches of the leather seat on either side of her; why did it seem to be her responsibility whether or not her father reclaimed his possessions? When would she stop having this power she did not wield? And then she said it. For the first time she said it aloud: "Why do you both blame everything on me?"

"You're reading it all wrong," he said quickly. "No one blames you for anything; don't take on more than belongs to you."

"Why didn't you come get your things? I would have felt a lot better." She listened to the dim, low noise of the car, the constant, even whir. It had taken her too long to recognize this, but cars were like elevators: you didn't get in them with anyone else, because then you were trapped, and cars and elevators were like certain subjects too. And all three of these things seemed characterized by low, menacing, constant noise.

"What do you mean, why didn't I come get my things?" He was yelling and then he slammed the palm of his hand against the steering wheel. "I didn't even know where you were for several months. You tell me about 'getting my things.' Tell me just how I was to do that. Who's laying blame here? And you certainly shouldn't be talking: you spend most of your time in a barn, for God's sake. A goddamn fucking barn."

IN HER OLD BEDROOM Mary had placed a blue vase stuffed full of sweet peas, their pink and white petals shaped like moth wings. The vase stood on a bedside table covered to the floor by a white cloth with a blue ruffle. The bed and the table were the only articles of furniture in the room and the table had not been there the last time she visited.

Something made her pull the white cloth up off the floor to see what was beneath it. "Accent Table will sustain 20 pounds of weight," was printed in block letters across the cardboard octagon. She let go of the hem of the tablecloth and it fell soundlessly back down to the floor.

She didn't quite know what she was feeling. Something about a piece of furniture being cardboard disturbed her— there was something hollow in it—or not hollow enough, as though perhaps she deserved only cardboard furniture. She felt silly for letting the cardboard table bother her, silly, and then ashamed for not feeling appreciative. She had returned to her old bedroom perhaps eight, maybe nine times and always she had had to place her things on the floor or on the window seat, and this lack of surfaces had embarrassed her, shamed her, as though she had defiled her room by taking from it her dressing table and her desk and the long library table with the legs carved to look like sheep's hooves. And now here was a small table, and even a blue vase with flowers, and she didn't want them, hated them in fact, as though they had been placed there in some very public way to announce her betrayal of this house, the house that had once been hers and her mother's and her father's and all of theirs together.

She could hear Mary moving around the kitchen, the sucking sound of the refrigerator being opened and shut, the chopping of a knife, her father's voice talking to Mary, their cool laughter mingling in the desultory jazz playing on the stereo.

One summer night long ago while her mother made dinner in that kitchen, dozens of white moths had clung to the screen door, their wings fluttering against the copper mesh, a static, still sort of music emanating from the screen. Now it seemed someone had gathered all those moths into their hands and made a bouquet of sweet pea blossoms to stand in a blue vase on this small cardboard table in her old bedroom.

Or perhaps it was all coincidence, the white moths on the screen, their static music, the blossoms in this blue vase— perhaps those two things weren't really connected at all except that they looked alike and reminded her of an evening long ago and of a moment right now and of her great loneliness in these thoughts and connections which were of no one else's mind but her own.

She hung her short-sleeved summer dresses in her old closet and paired her shoes beneath them. She placed a couple of small stuffed bears on the bed. She put a stack of books on the new night table under the sweet peas and their curling tendrils. In the dim, even light from the wall sconces the tendrils cast a shadow like wrought iron across the books. She heard the floor creak very quietly and then Mary stood in the doorway, the dark curls around her face like a thick hood.

"Settled?" Mary asked.

"Thank you for the flowers."

"Sure. *Lathyrus odoratus.*"

"What?"

"Oh, nothing, just their official name. A bad habit, like practicing for a test. Hungry?"

"Sure. I guess."

"I have some odd vegetables. Squash that is half crookneck and half zucchini. Sometimes we get bored in the lab."

"Are you sure we should eat them?" There was a dim shore of light around Mary's head in the doorway. It had been a year since she had seen her. She thought of hugging Mary with happiness and affection, wanted to, yet this seemed somehow unfair to her mother, an effrontery even, to hug the woman who was now in her mother's kitchen, who now slept in her mother's old bedroom. When Mary and she had first met in the hallway earlier this evening she had approached Mary with awkward hesitation, and then had embraced her quickly, disjointedly. She felt embarrassed by her lack of smoothness, of grace. She knew from past years that the tension would subside gradually but at first it was substantial and unrelenting; her mother seemed to be watching her every move and gesture, as though Elisabeth were still in fact there in the old house, her face and torso in each corner of a room at the top of the walls like coving or a cornice, bearing down upon the room and its occupants.

"It won't hurt you to eat them; they're just squash, silly. May I come in?" Her heel tapped softly on the hardwood flooring.

"Sure. Of course." She felt a pang of guilt or stupidity or shame—there was perhaps no specific name for it. It was just awkwardness—always awkwardness—and her sense that she couldn't ever catch up to what was really going on. Her mother had never paused before entering her room, and it wasn't that her mother was impolite, no, it was just understood between them that her mother's presence in her daughter's room was desired, permissible, even rather unconditional. For the first time in her life she wondered about this, and thought of her father in the car saying she didn't even know what her mother was doing to her. And of David at the festival ball saying she'd learned not to miss people from her mother, her beautiful mother, whom he claimed she didn't even know.

What was her mother doing to her? She liked it that her mother felt comfortable enough to come into her bedroom; she didn't really want her mother knocking, acting like a butler at the threshold of her door. Not that Mary was acting like a butler, she was just being polite. But no, there was more than politeness to Mary's hesitation; there was separation: she, Lisa, was a person separate from others, a person who not only had but deserved the power of her will, her desire. For a moment she breathed a new form of air, easing, freeing, and almost in the same instant she felt the remove of formality, the good, clear wall all around her. And the loneliness.

"How have you been, Lisa? How's your bladder problem?"

"I'm really fine," she said. "Really." A plane flew low over-head; she raised her head slightly to listen; it was the old habit. "I guess Dad's at home, isn't he?"

"I do it too," Mary said. "I can't tell you the number of times I've run out to the driveway, made a complete and utter fool of myself waving, and then Neville's come home and said, 'No, I didn't buzz the house today. Somebody up there's getting a lot of ground attention.' "

"Did Dad ever tell you about flying over that section of the Oakland hills where all the women sunbathe in the nude?"

"Oh, no matter where the boys are flying they detour over there," Mary said, rolling her eyes.

"Do you think they can really see from that altitude?"

"I think it's more like going to the wild animal park: they want to see women in their natural habitat. It doesn't really matter if they're far away. There's some allure in that. Plus, though they're not big on admitting this, they have bin-oculars."

"I never thought of that. But, of course, they would, wouldn't they?"

"They would." Mary and she were silent for a beat and then Lisa broke the silence just before it became awkward.

"Thank you for the little nightstand," she said. "It's nice to have some place to put books."

"Why don't you come and stay with us and we'll get you some real furniture. How about your senior year of high school?"

She was taken off guard. Of the questions she could have anticipated, this was not one. "Your father would be very pleased, you know." She wondered if Mary knew for a fact that he would be pleased should she come to visit for longer than a few weeks every year. "Next year? Right, that's your senior year?"

"Yes, next year."

"And maybe the choice of guys will be better here. You never know." Mary laughed.

"He's really worried about me not having a boyfriend, isn't he? Tell him there's nothing wrong with me, will you?" She could hear her father changing the music in the living room, the sound of the cellophane on the album cover, and the short pause before the first musical notes, and then the dull clap of the wooden door on the stereo cabinet.

"I already did."

"Oh."

"He doesn't like the fact that you don't have a boyfriend, nor, let me add"—Mary was whispering—"does he like it that your mother's friend is younger than she is."

"What does David have to do with anything? Dad doesn't even know him. I like David. I like him a lot; and I missed him."

"What do you mean, you missed him?"

"He was in Saudi Arabia for a while."

"What's 'a while'?"

"Two years. He went to build a palace."

"Just be careful. That's all Neville wants."

"Paranoid—both of my parents!"

"They love you."

"That's a possibility, isn't it?" she said, laughing easily, but then stopping herself. "But what is the problem? Huh? David is my mother's friend. But even still, what if he were my *boy*friend? What would it matter? Why would that be so bad? Anyway, he seems to say the same things to me that Dad does: Your mother's doing this to you, your mother's doing that to you."

"Lisa, just don't listen to them. Men always perceive the worst in women who've rejected them. It's de rigueur."

"What's that mean?"

"It's obligatory," Mary said.

"I wouldn't know if it was obligatory or not," Neville said, leaning up against the doorjamb. "With Elisabeth I'd say it's necessary, however."

"We didn't know you were there," Mary said.

"Nor do you really know what you're talking about when it comes to Elisabeth," he said, trying to force a smile across his face. "I happen to have lived with her for twelve years."

"Could we not talk about Mom?" she said, pulling the closet doors shut, listening for that old familiar click of the metal plates as they met in the middle.

"Maybe it's high time we did talk about her. I can't see that she's doing you any favors. I want you to come and live here next year—to have other influences."

She looked at him standing casually in the doorway, his stockinged feet crossed at the ankle. She had almost been flattered by the offer.

"What he means is that he'd like to have more time with you," Mary said. "There's always so little time. And soon you'll be in college."

"Do I always need an interpreter, Mary? She knows what

I mean. I want her to come live with us; it's as simple as that."

"Nothing is simple, Neville," Mary said, starting to move back through the doorway. "And she knows that better than any of you," she murmured under her breath.

"What's so very difficult about her coming to live with us for a year? You pack a few bags and say goodbye—or she doesn't even have to pack her bags, for Christ's sake—we'll buy her whatever she needs." He had now uncrossed his feet and was leaning his face into Mary as she passed through the door. Lisa watched him follow her with his eyes, and then he looked at the floor and sighed deeply. "That was a stupid thing to say: I know we can't buy you everything you need, but at least you won't have to put your fist through a window to get into your own house. What do you say?"

The room with its hardwood floors and its lack of furniture acted as a type of echo chamber into which these words had been spoken. They seemed to take on a shrill life of their own, as though each word were a battery-driven toy suddenly switched on and careering about.

"Neville," Mary said from the living room. "Why don't we sit down to dinner."

He didn't move from the doorway. "What do you say?" he asked again. She saw him standing in the courthouse cafeteria taking her tray from her, telling her that they were over at a table against the wall. She remembered the din of the cafeteria, could hear it here in her old bedroom. She remembered the lawyers and the judge: You're a lucky little girl—not many children get to choose which parent they want to live with. "Come on, baby, one year, that's all I'm asking. She's had you for five years—I've had you for a few lousy weeks." She could feel his tears on her forehead as they got off the elevator and his angry pronouncement that Elisabeth had won everything, even the fur coat fund, everything.

There seemed to be many more battery-driven toys careering

around her old bedroom, bumping into one another, hitting her feet and ankles, their tinny bodies clamoring across the floor into the bedposts, or into the closet doors or the paneling below the window seat.

"Please at least say something," he almost whispered. "I'm not sure I can handle this twice in one lifetime."

She took air into her lungs as though she were about to speak, but no words came out.

"At least say you'll think about it," he said, as though he had read her mind. "At least think about it on your own, with no one else influencing you."

"I will—"

The telephone rang once and then her father straightened up, said "Thank you" very quietly, and walked from the doorway out across the living-room carpet.

She wandered around her room, the boards sounding pliant and meek beneath her footsteps. She wouldn't mind living here again, she thought. She wouldn't mind the quiet isolation of this house, or spending a long period of time in her old bedroom with the window seat and the grove of baby eucalyptus trees outside its windows. She wouldn't mind talking with Mary—maybe even growing comfortable with her—no, she wouldn't mind any of that. But all she could see in her bare room was the empty house five years ago and the plains of dust which glistened in the sunlight as the movers lifted a couch from the area or a bureau—all she could see was the look on her father's face when he stepped onto the tile entry that evening—and herself stretched across the back seat of the Mercury, warming her feet on the back windows, saying nothing, doing nothing, just going along, being a kid.

"Lisa, the phone's for you," Mary said, standing once again in the doorway. "You can take it in our bedroom, okay?"

It had to be her mother; only her mother and Maria knew where she was, and she was sure Maria wouldn't call her until tomorrow or the next day, when Maria's parents were at work and they could talk on the telephone for as long as they wanted.

"Just tell me when you pick up the receiver so I can hang it up in the kitchen," Mary said.

She wasn't surprised that it was her mother. Her mother had that knack of being everywhere. She crossed the living room knowing Elisabeth was there in the floor and in the ceiling and in the layers of eggshell-white paint on the walls.

The master bedroom looked very different now: clean, modern, rudimentary, perhaps even a little stark. But Elisabeth was there in the paned doors that had been knocked through to the garden.

"Thanks, Mary, I have it," she said, and waited for the series of thumps and clicks that meant the phone had been hung up in the kitchen. "Hi, Mom."

"It's not your mom," he said. She could see him pushing his blond hair back from his face.

"David, what are you doing calling? How did you get this number?"

"What do you mean, how did I get this number? It's listed; any moron can get it."

"Oh."

"I'm driving over your way on Wednesday to see a building site, so I thought maybe I could take you to lunch?"

"Oh, well, okay."

"Show some enthusiasm—"

"I am, I mean I will—I'm just surprised."

"Good, you need some surprises. So, I'll call you Wednesday morning and then you'll have to give me directions."

"Does Mom know about this?"

"I'll talk to you on Wednesday, okay?" He waited a second for her response, and then hung up slowly. She could hear water running in the walls of the house. She felt excited, flattered—it was romantic; it was secret: nobody knew, nobody could say anything, could control anything or puncture it. She went to the kitchen, where it smelled of garlic and olive oil and candles burning. They were drinking wine the color of straw and waiting for her, the platter of sweet peppers and pear-shaped zucchini laid down long sleeves of bread, shining in the light of the tiny flames.

"I thought you didn't have a boyfriend," her father said. "But the truth emerges." He smiled kindly.

"He's not my boyfriend. What a silly word anyway!" He hadn't recognized David's voice; she felt intensely heartened by this.

"Then who is he?" he asked, slipping a server under one of the slices of bread and lifting it to her plate.

"Just a friend, Dad."

"What's his name?"

"Privacy, what a concept," Mary said, pulling her napkin out from under her fork. "Come on, Neville, she'll tell you when she wants to."

"If I waited for this one to tell me something on her own, I'd never know anything. How'd he get this number anyway?"

"It's listed; any moron can get it—"

"So, this guy's a moron—"

"I don't think the telephone got hung up all the way, Neville. Would you mind getting that?"

"How can you hear that? I can't hear a thing." He pushed back from the table, the chair legs scraping on the tile. Lisa hadn't noticed either, but now that she listened she could detect the high-pitched whine coming from their bedroom.

"I'm sorry. I thought I hung it up."

"You did. It just has to sit in the cradle in a certain way," Mary said, and walked out of the kitchen after Neville. Just before their bedroom door closed solidly, Lisa heard Mary raise her voice in astonishment, "I can't believe—" and then her voice disappeared in the sound of the door meeting the doorjamb, that single thudding note of impact, and afterward, her voice audible but muffled, as turbulent as strong wind beyond the walls of a barn.

She picked the server up from the platter and dished Mary and her father's plates. She didn't work carefully or quickly enough and so there was a dribble of olive oil leading from either end of the platter; amber cobblestones, petrified resin, the way pointed out in the forest with bread crumbs, the way lapped up by a hungry squirrel, or maybe a rain heavy enough to dissolve olive oil, or a great wind shaking the trees, their leaves showering down, covering the golden droplets. She wiped up the table with her napkin. She switched their wineglasses, Mary's fuller glass now at her father's place, and her father's glass now at Mary's. She thought of the worst possible things that could happen—airplane crashes, mutilation, her mother's hands sawed off, Mary killed. She felt better because if she could think of something, then it couldn't happen.

IN HER BARE FEET she walked so quietly she couldn't hear herself move. They had left her a long note on the kitchen table. Morning light and a place setting of silverware held it down. She could see both Mary's round, candid writing and her father's rather belabored hand. She circled the table, roving her hand up and over the four chair backs. The faucet dripped just as her hand reached the center of each curved rail. She smelled the citrus of dish detergent and the faint odor of garlic. She pulled the refrigerator door open and then let it swing shut. Her shoulders fell. She made a deal with herself that she didn't have to read the note till three o'clock—unless, of course, the telephone rang and then she would have to dash through it in case the call was from them. She smiled, relief budding in her face, her shoulders, and her knuckles. Six hours before three o'clock, six long silent hours. She moved her hand along the counter edges, up and over the front of the oven and the broom closet and down to the back door and to the doorknob. It was a globe in her hand, a tiny world, six hours' worth.

She walked up and down the rows of Mary's garden, the soil warm beneath her feet, her soles particularly sensitive, her attention in her arches and heels and in the delighted coves between her toes. She was alone; she could feel her body, could feel the air and the allspice of the eucalyptus rush its way down into her chest and heart and abdomen. The air smelled like happiness, was happiness, was energy and transportation and sleep. She sat on the ground in the garden for an hour, perhaps two, she didn't know. It didn't matter. She watched the breeze move the leaves across the ground as though trying to arrange them among the twigs and pebbles into some sort of ancient rebus; she watched the momentary shudder of a branch after a sparrow lifted from it; she watched a large bug on its back, a beetle perhaps, being stung by hundreds of ants so small she counted eight of them lined up along the bug's leg. The bug continued to twitch and every so often buzzed. She wasn't sure she felt sickened by the scene; there was a harshness in the world she supposed natural. Her mind wandered; a poppy tossed its orange petals in a cancan with the wind; her mother sat alone at the breakfast table in Sonoma. Elisabeth had set a place for her, had set out a milk glass and her rabbit napkin ring, had set a fork and spoon and knife alongside the smooth white plate. A runnel of sweat ran down between her breasts to the waistband of her pajamas and she realized the sun had gotten hot. If she looked up into the sun for a long enough time, she would go blind, would be in a hospital with her head wrapped around with a broad white bandage. They would have to take care of her, they would feel sorry for her and pity her. She got up and walked back through a row of Mary's garden, and even though the tin plant markers each had two Latin names written across them in black grease pencil, she recognized the spiraled, hoary canes of squash plants, the green radish leaf tongues and carrot fronds and the tall thistles of artichokes.

She sat in her window seat reading a Raymond Chandler novel she'd found on her father's bookshelves. On the cover there was a lake with a woman's hand coming up out of the water and nearby on a pier stood two men, one in a suit and hat and the other in a blue shirt, looking as though they were about to fight. She was supposed to be reading *Tess of the D'Urbervilles*, but she had gotten to the part where Angel Clare marries Tess and they are supremely happy for a few hours until they confess their past lives. Tess forgives him his fling with a London whore, but Tess's rape and child are not forgivable in Clare's eyes: she has become a different person. She hated Angel Clare and found her jaw clenched shut and her head aching. She could scream at him right here and now in her room; Chandler read simply, matter-of-factly, safely; she didn't put herself in the book, she merely wanted to know what happened. Marlowe moved stealthily, assuredly, she didn't have to worry about him. Even when he got knocked out or drugged, it was something you knew he could handle.

At three o'clock she read the note on the kitchen table. She put the silverware in the sink so that they would think she'd used it. She swept the kitchen floor the way Mary had asked and pulled the chicken from the freezer to defrost. She submerged it in very hot water, hoping it would thaw by the time they came home. She didn't think about living here next year as her father had suggested; she pushed it out of her mind, "released it to the universe," as a movie star said in a magazine she read once. Finally she made herself get dressed, the shorts and shirt feeling tight, binding, though they did not fit her snugly.

DAVID CALLED AT 11:20 on Wednesday morning. She was sitting in the window seat reading a collection of short stories by Colette when she heard the jangle of the telephone. She gave him directions to the house mostly with landmarks instead of street names and highways and then told him to park beneath the trees, the denser ones nearer the back of the drive. She could hear the reservation in his voice, the slight pause, and then his silent acquiescence; she kept imagining her father flying over and seeing a car that she would later have to explain.

She had been dressed fifteen minutes after Mary and her father left for work, and then she had taken her dress off and laid it across the bed so she wouldn't wrinkle it. That was two hours ago, two and a half really. She looked from her blue dress laid neatly across the bed to her book sitting like a tiny tent on the cushions of the window seat. The book was a taut but neat world between covers; her dress was acute, high, invigorating, a smooth sheath at her waist, its blue a small sky from which her eyes caught a hue that pleased her, made her think well of herself—made her think herself almost desirable. And then instantly her excitement changed to misgiving: how had she gotten herself into this? David was her mother's friend. Why was he calling her and taking her to lunch when Elisabeth didn't even know? It was happening, she thought; it was just happening.

She stepped into her dress, careful not to catch the heel of her shoe in the hem, her mother's voice in her head telling her not to be so lazy, to take her shoes off before she did that. This afternoon was for her, she thought—her life was about to begin.

She stood in the sunlight watering the potted plants along the front of the house when he arrived and parked just as she had told him to. It was warm outside, that clear deep sunlight of late summer, early autumn. She hadn't felt its intensity till now.

"Afraid of your dad, huh?" he said, getting out of his red Alpine, which looked to her like a small rodent.

"That's not the way I'd put it."

"Then how would you put it?" He leaned down and kissed her on the cheek. She wanted him to kiss her again, on the other cheek, the way Europeans kissed when they were happy. But he was already looking away at the plants she had watered. "Will you help me with my garden in Sonoma? The renters left a mess."

"I guess so. I don't really have much talent at it." She watched him look around the drive and up at the roofline of the house and then past her through the front door standing open and lighted by a diagonal of sunlight.

"Great houses they built in the thirties."

"If it will generate questions, I try to avoid it." Her sentence sounded mature to her and intelligent; she felt very much in possession of herself, and thin, her stomach empty, her mind anxious, alert.

He looked at her puzzled. "Oh, the car you mean. That's coy," he said. "Show me this house?"

"It's not coy. You don't understand if you think I'm being coy. Do you have to answer a barrage of questions every time you do something or say something or want anything?"

"Barrage. You really have your mother's vocabulary—and that's good. Don't get me wrong, that is good. And as for the 'Do I get the old third degree?'—of course I do. My mother should have been a trial attorney; she could break down a corpse with her questioning."

She took him through the living room and the kitchen, out onto the patio and into the garden—into Mary's mini-laboratory—back into the house to the master bedroom and then back across the living room toward her room. Sunlight made the house bright, made the dust particles on the end tables sparkle like fool's gold in a shallow stream.

"All this built-in stuff is just terrific," he said. He pulled out a long, wide board beneath the linen closet cupboards that she could see her mother standing before, folding towels and sheets, doing deep knee bends to the wicker basket for a pillowcase or a hand towel, her housework and exercise regimen combined.

"My father wants me to come live here next year—for my senior year of high school."

"I don't think you should do that." He walked to the window seat, as everyone did who entered her bedroom, and looked out the window onto the drive. He then looked down at her book and the several cushions along the seat and up against the walls of the alcove. "Did you know Colette's husband used to keep her locked up in a room all day so that she would write?"

"Which husband? She had three."

She watched his back shrug almost imperceptibly. "Oh," he said, his tone a mixture of sarcasm and fatigue. "Well, I suppose it doesn't really matter, does it?" He turned the handle on the window and one of the vertical iron rods moved down from inside the casement and one up from inside the sill. "I don't think your mother would ever forgive you." His back remained to her; she sat on the corner of her bed. "And I probably wouldn't either," he said quietly, twisting the window handle, the iron rods moving back into place.

He turned to look at her, as though she were to respond, but she couldn't imagine what to say. Now, somehow, in a matter of days, David too had become another person in her life to choose for or against.

"You never answered my question about Mom. Does she know you're here?" The answer to this question now had all to do with Sonoma: would she stay there her senior year for her mother and David, or for her mother and for David?

"In fact, she does know I'm here. I managed to persuade her that taking you to lunch was an innocent and rather paternal activity."

"Yeah, it is," she said, getting up from the bed. "It's very paternal." Lunches are paternal activities, she said beneath her breath.

"What?" he asked absently, turning back to the window.

"I just agreed with you that lunches are the acts of fathers."

"I never realized you were so cynical. Or that you had become . . ."

She didn't like being called cynical; she associated it with meanness; she didn't want to be mean. She didn't answer him or retort. They were both quiet.

"So, this is what you left," he finally said. He turned and looked at her closely.

"I suppose—"

"Or rather—what your mother left."

She hesitated before speaking. "I guess we both left it . . . really."

"I know the story, Lisa—"

"Oh, do you?" There was an edge in her voice which she couldn't control.

"I mean that I know a version of the story. I don't blame you for being—"

"I'm not angry. But why are we talking about this?" Why are you here? she wanted to blurt out.

"I didn't know you before you came to Sonoma. You were different, I bet. I wish I'd known you then—"

"I was a little kid—what's there to know?" He sat down in the window seat and began to stack his lap with cushions.

"A lot." He pulled the last cushion out from under him and added this to the stack. She hadn't remembered the wood of the window seat. Walnut. She knew it was walnut, but it had been years since she'd seen it. She used to slide her hand down behind the back pillow to feel the smooth, slightly waxy surface, her fingers moving slowly in an attempt to trace the pattern of the grain. She hadn't done that in years. He perched the Colette atop the stack and looked at her through the triangular aperture it made. "You must have been different."

"That's why you're here? To find . . ." She sat back down on the bed. She thought of her stuffed bears concealed in the closet before he came.

"Not so elliptical," he said, looking out at her over the binding.

She struggled for an instant with "elliptical," one of those words she kept having to look up, eclipse and ellipse superimposing each other. She eyed her dictionary on the floor, half hidden by the blue ruffle of the tablecloth. "That's why you're here?"

"No, I'm here to look at a building site, remember?" She wondered if in fact there was a building site; maybe he'd made it up. She would save him from having to continue this pretense; she wanted him here just for her.

"What does your castle look—"

"Palace, not castle; palace." The rush of an airplane overhead enveloped the room. They looked at each other across the huge sound, he over the volume of stories now turned sideways, Colette's hard face staring out at her, the one eye obscured by bobbed, frazzled hair, the other deep within a socket so dark with fatigue or sorrow or bitterness it looked like an eye patch, even though the eye looked steadily from its center.

"Did you meet people in Saudi Arabia?" she asked.

"You mean, did I meet women in Saudi?"

"Are you and Mother back together again?"

"English women primarily. Very blond, very pretty, but of course just as confined by Muslim law as the Arab women—"

"Why won't you answer that question?"

"No, we're not. Okay?"

"But you were the other night—why aren't you now?" She looked at Colette's face resting on the liver-spotted hand, although sideways it looked more as if a fist were moving in from the right to clip her chin. Then he righted the book, thumbing through its pages; Colette peered at her, the dissipation of her face and eyes in contrast with the hard fist beneath her chin and the chintz curtain flounced elegantly above her head.

"Your mother doesn't want me—hasn't for years," he said.

Her face flushed hot. "Maybe we should go?" He replaced the cushions in the window seat, the Colette wedged under his arm.

"I think I've lost your place." He set the book down carefully. "Do you have an idea?"

"I think you wanted to lose my place," she said, happy—almost anxious—to tease him, to soothe her mother's rejection of him.

"I'm not sure I know—"

"Oh, you know, you know."

"No, I don't," he said impatiently. "I don't think I do know; let's go."

She edged her way toward the doorway. "I didn't mean to—"

"I'm not here necessarily for reasons." He walked into the center of the room.

"I just thought you were here for . . ." she whispered, wishing herself as invisible as when the blue dress had lain across the bed, flat, empty.

"Lisa. I'm not—" The room was very quiet for a moment; and then all she could hear was the sound of his shoes walking across the floor. "I'm sorry if you got the wrong idea."

"I'm not a child," she said. "I haven't gotten the wrong idea."

"No, you aren't really, are you?" He stood over her with a look on his face she wanted to scratch off: concerned, sympathetic, unflinchingly honorable. "Where are we off to for lunch?" He put his arm around her shoulder and led her from the bedroom. It wasn't his fault, she thought. Although she wanted to blame him, it wasn't his fault at all.

HE PULLED THE PAPER SHEATH off the narrow strip of bamboo which when split made chopsticks. He sanded one stick with the side of the other, the splinters dusting down upon the black lacquer tray before him. The veins stood out on the backs of his hands. They were big hands, or not big but long, she thought. He reached for her chopsticks, split them quickly, expertly, the thin pieces of bamboo almost entirely lost within his palms as he planed one stick across the other. He handed them over without looking at her, his face turned up toward the sushi chef. Her nose was almost level with his shoulder and she felt diminutive next to him, tiny and fragile and protected—his body strong and tall and buffering; she wasn't hungry; she would do anything to preserve this smallness, this lovely compactness she felt being at the side of his body. She wouldn't eat. She wouldn't destroy this.

"*Tekka maki. Himachi. Uni*—just one order of those. *Toro*—two. *Ikura*, one order—with quail egg. *Hirami*. And just one order of *tamago*. We'll see how far that gets us."

She looked before her at the raw filets of salmon and albacore and yellowtail, and at a mound of shrimp next to a basket of speckled eggs no bigger than malted-milk balls. Along the front of the vitrine stretched an octopus tentacle with its two rows of tiny mouths sucking the glass. "You've never had sushi before?" he was asking her. "I can hardly believe that. Are you sure?" She could see through the glass to the narrow wooden counter where the chef with a harsh sort of intensity patted down a rectangle of sticky white rice.

"I think I would remember eating raw fish."

"Oh, raw—stop with the raw business. You're talking like

people talk who don't know anything about it, as if raw were the only characteristic it had." But he was goading her gently, an amused glint in his eye. "It's like calling the Taj Mahal white."

The sushi chef handed down two square dishes, which David took, placing one on her tray and one on his. Each dish had a pile of pickled ginger the color of shell cameos and a mound of green paste in which she could see an intaglio of the chef's thumbprint.

"*Wasabi,*" he said. He mixed soy sauce and a small bit of the paste in a shallow bowl with his chopsticks. The chef handed down a wooden board mounded up like a tiny Stonehenge. "All right, here begins the maiden voyage," and he picked off a piece of pale crimson sushi, dipped it in the sauce, and moved it toward her mouth, passing it so quickly and smoothly into her she could do nothing but take it, the cool, buttery texture as soft as an earlobe, the taste of the ocean and of sea spray and of something hot opening her sinuses, making her breathe deeply, fully, the thrill in her chest like sudden fear. He smiled at her.

"Oh—"

"Hot?"

A waiter brought a slender glass of beer and set it before David. The chef leaned across and knocked a quail egg lightly against the glass's rim. He pulled the mottled shells apart, the yolk making a slow descent down the column of pale beer. "For strength. Man strength," the chef said, and bowed quickly, the bluish white of his scalp showing through the black crew-cut hair.

David raised his glass to his mouth, waiting, not drinking, sucking really, the egg rising up the glass like the sun until he gulped and the yellow yolk disappeared past his lips.

"YOU'RE LEAVING TOMORROW and you haven't answered me about next year." Neville spoke quietly, his head angled down. "You might want to consider longer, I don't know, but why don't you just decide on coming here next year?"

The question had been in the air for two weeks now, hovering with a slowly increasing intensity—but she had not expected it at this moment, his car idling, the morning barely arrived, his hand draped over the stick shift just ready to pull it back into reverse. She had not expected it getting quietly out of bed, tiptoeing anxiously across the floor for her robe, excited to surprise him with a goodbye as he drove off before the birds had begun to stir. She'd expected the question that evening at dinner, but not at this moment in which she had been wholly unguarded, happy to send him off, the high feeling of having shown him care sinking down behind her eyes into her throat where it solidified and became as snug as a cork stopper.

"Look, I know I've put you in a tough position, but come on, baby, be fair."

"Dad, it's not really my decision. I think you know that."

"Of course it's your decision—why shouldn't it be?" He wobbled the stick shift to make sure it was in neutral and then got out of the car. "It *is* your decision."

"I don't know, I mean, I do know." She could feel the gravel of the drive through her slippers. "I think she'd take you to court—both of us—to court. I don't think she'd stand for it."

"But it wouldn't be her decision—you're old enough now, the judge would listen to you; it's up to you. It is." He looked straight at her now, his eyes dark and unreadable. "It's your decision and you're just refusing to make it."

What does it cost you to make this decision? she wanted to say to him—to scream at him—but this impulse surged at the same time as she wanted so very much to make this decision for him, to make him readable again, to make him forget the empty house he had returned to that night, the emptiness she had helped create by her silence—by her inability to make a decision.

"How would I tell her? Huh, Dad? What would I say? 'Hey, Mom, I don't want to live with you any longer.' Is that what I'd say?" She was terrified he'd bring up the past, terrified he'd say, Well, you didn't have any problem a few years ago telling a judge you didn't want to live with me. But instead he was calm, almost gentle.

"Sure, why not. What does it matter? Come on, baby, I just want to have some time with you—time in which we're not snarking at each other." He put his hand on hers and pulled her toward him. "It seems so little to ask, but then maybe it isn't. I don't know. Tell me soon, okay? Just tell me soon." He dropped himself onto the car seat and was gone down the drive as quickly as a bullet is moved into a chamber and down a barrel. She watched after him, after the car, her neck and shoulders rigid, the morning fresh and simple about her, dew in the air, and the birds just beginning to exchange the frantic, candid chatter of their lives.

SHE HEARD HER MOTHER'S CAR on the gravel. She stood in her bedroom in the lozenge of light from the leaded window and could see into the drive. The Mercury seemed older, duller, its red paint dusty as a stop sign on a rural road. She heard the tail end of a newscast as her mother stepped from the car and then the metal of the car and the car's door meshing shut.

She was alone. Mary was "in the field," as she said, in Oregon, researching the effects of excessive moisture on certain crops, and her father had left for work an hour earlier. He was going to fly Arnold Amis, the Bacon King, into the Canadian tundra, because he wanted to kill a moose, her father had told her—he wanted a rack of antlers in his study upon which he could suspend a nude woman during a bachelor party he was throwing for his oldest son. And the Bacon King

wanted the velvet still hanging from the antlers in long sugges-
tive shreds, he wanted the velvet from the antlers to seem as
if it were molting right off the woman. "Of course," her father
said, "it was too late for that." In the spring moose rubbed
the velvet off against the bark of trees; but they were going
anyway.

Her father explained all this to her as if she were going
with them to the tundra, or as if she had something integral
to do with the festivities of the bachelor party. She felt that
her father wanted her to be amused, to laugh, to join in, but
what interested her primarily was the thin blanket of fur called
velvet which covered the antlers. She thought of the expression
"an iron fist in a velvet glove." She wondered if this expression
fit the moose she could see standing in a clump of sparse
shrubs chewing pensively, his great dewlaps hanging below
his slow mouth, moving like the loose upper arms of old
women.

She thought of power and powerlessness. Alone, one on
one, her father was no match for a moose, and a moose stood
no chance against the scoped rifle she had watched her father
clean carefully the night before. What if the moose had the
scope and could detect where the hunters crouched, and the
hunters merely had a rifle which would dip and sway with
the nervousness of their eager eyes? What if the wind blew so
fiercely across the hard ice that the hunters' arms could not
steady their heavy weapons?

In her mind she tried to keep the moose alive, but it kept
falling before her, its knobby legs crumpling into the shrubs,
which crackled as though on fire. She saw the moose die slowly,
quietly and with a dignity which sickened her. His great head
was sinking and his antlers tangled with the low shrub into a
network like a throw of pick-up-sticks made from twigs.

Not even her imagination could keep the moose alive. She
had always thought the one power she possessed was thought,

was perception, which she could deny or embellish to her liking. But the moose was dying and what remained seemed at once imperturbable and menacing: the dead moose and the low gray brush and the stone antlers—all tangled and inert.

Her mother tried her key in the front door and when it failed to work started to push at the door and clang the door knocker. Lisa's cases stood in the entry hall so there would be no reason for her mother to enter the house. Her father had made sure of that. Yet what if her mother persisted? What would she say, and what if her mother just walked straight in without asking, how would she stop her without making her angry? And she would be angry. The door knocker banged several times in succession and finally she walked through the living room to answer it. For a moment she forgot her father's instruction and thrilled at the prospect of being with her mother again, of being once more within her humor and gaiety, and when she pulled the door open the sun behind her mother backlit her as though she were on stage, a huge star waiting for the applause she knew was sure to come.

"Hello sweetheart hello sweetheart hello sweetheart." It was her mother's pearly voice, smooth and milky and beautiful, and her mother's arms, which smelled of spice and raspberries, were around her, holding her in the darkness between her breasts. But when she pulled away, her hair caught around the large buttons and she could not help but think of the moose, chewing stupidly, placidly alone in the tundra, the moose that now lay in the lap of his own great throat. Her mother walked on into the living room and sat on the back of a white leather couch.

"So, how are you, sweetheart?" she asked, adjusting the strap of her shoe. "I've missed you—so has the rose garden, the fig tree, and the house too groans occasionally and asks in a deep, stern voice when you're coming back, and now I've got you once again."

"I'm fine," she said, smiling. It was useless to resist her mother. Rarely did anyone try. It would have been like turning over and dumping out pots of flowers.

"He certainly hasn't done very well on furnishings, has he? What a hideous couch."

"It's cool when it's hot, though."

"I suppose if you like sticking to things," her mother said, walking to the master bedroom. She opened the door and walked in. Lisa could hear the tap of her shoes on the hardwood floor. She knew she should follow her, watch her, she knew she wasn't supposed to let her in, to let her "case the joint" as her father had put it, but her mother was opening the medicine cabinets in the bathroom, and then the closet doors were being drawn open and hangers were sliding across the rods.

For a moment there was no sound but the wind rattling the leaves in the drive and then her mother appeared in the doorway with her hands in her pockets, smiling, her head tilted.

"Shouldn't we go?" Lisa asked. "I mean, it's kind of a long drive."

"In a moment. I need something to drink first. What's your father keeping nowadays?"

Her mother was in the kitchen before she could think of what to answer or to say to make her leave sooner. She hadn't heard the closet doors in the master bedroom being shut and she knew she would have to somehow get them closed so that her father would not know Elisabeth had been in the house. She followed her mother into the kitchen and watched her pull out drawer after drawer. Some she shut, others she rummaged within and just left open. Her mother turned and looked up at an iron pot rack suspended over the stove and then, leaning against the tile counter, folded her arms and asked, "Did he buy you any clothes?"

"No," she said. Her mother gazed steadily at the pot rack. It was very quiet until Lisa pulled open the refrigerator door and bottles and jars knocked solidly against the insulated plastic interior. And then it was very quiet again. "Do you want a beer?" she asked.

"Why not?"

"Why not what?" she asked.

"Why didn't he buy you any clothes? I told you he was to buy you some clothes. German knives. Copper pots. He can buy you some clothes."

"But I didn't need any clothes," she said very softly and then added, "did I?"

"You're goddamn right you needed clothes. The shit he pays for child support. You had one thing to attend to the entire two weeks you were here, young lady. One thing I asked you to do. Just one thing." Her mother pushed away from the counter and walked toward the refrigerator. She drew a beer bottle from a side shelf and slammed the door shut. "One goddamn thing."

"But we don't need to ask him for money, Mom. We don't need it."

"He owes you support, Lisa. Just because *my* father made some wise investments doesn't mean *your* father's off the hook. Why should he be? Think about it, hmm, why?"

"I think we better go now," she said. "I just think we better go."

"Where are the pilsner glasses?" Elisabeth asked. She pulled open cupboard doors until she found one and then, after twisting the bottle cap off with a dish towel, poured the bottle's contents into the conical glass and walked into the entry hall and out the front door, which closed with a clank of the door knocker.

She felt the acid swelling in her stomach. There was also the twinge and burn at the small of her back. She walked slowly about the kitchen closing drawers and cupboards. She put the bottle cap in the trash, making sure it dropped down below other trash, and rehung the dish towel on the oven door handle. The kitchen looked the way she and her father had left it earlier in the morning; except it didn't look that way at all. Her father would realize Elisabeth had gone through his closets. He would sense it. She hoped he would not mention it to her, and yet, why shouldn't he mention it, why shouldn't he be angry about his ex-wife going through what was now his house, his home?

She turned from the kitchen and went into the master bedroom. The closet doors all stood ajar. She quickly closed them and went into the bathroom, where she switched off the light and closed the cabinets. Her father's electric razor lay on the counter near his cologne. In the dimness she picked up the bottle and smelled the campfire of oak logs burning with limes and lemons; this was his smell and she would not smell it for several months to come. She daubed the back of her hand with cologne just as the Mercury's horn blasted long and hard. She froze for an instant and then left the bathroom and then the bedroom, pulling the door shut behind her.

She found a space for the bottle in the bag with her books and her stuffed animals. It rested there surrounded by plastic-button faces and the stack of old paperback Hemingway novels her father had given her. Their covers depicted scenes which she could not seem to find within the text of the books. She could not find the romantic love that the covers promised, or the great manes of dark Latino hair. In fact, weren't they always blondes? But if it was on the book's cover, surely the book had it somewhere, surely the book had a woman with huge breasts in it somewhere.

She picked up her two cases and walked with them to the car. Her mother did not seem to be around. The bag with the cologne remained in the hallway and she returned for this and held it tightly against her chest as though it were a pillow. She settled it in the back seat on the floor, careful not to cover the hole in the floorboard through which she could see a slender leaf embedded in the gravel of the drive. She walked back to the house and closed the heavy front door; the knocker chinked lightly. She checked the door to make sure it was locked, and as she turned around came face to face with her mother.

"Let's go," Elisabeth said. "Let's go have lunch on your father."

She watched her mother walk to the car. Her mother was holding the pilsner glass and then she was positioning it between the seats; she knew her mother had no intention of returning it. At her feet the wind fluttered eucalyptus leaves and she thought maybe the wind was a great bird under whose wings the land always was, and when the great bird settled itself, moving its wings once or twice to get them comfortable, then of course what depended and subsisted upon the land also moved and settled in order to quiet the great bird. Yes, she thought, the wind was an immense transparent bird but someday she would see it, would know to stroke it and make it do what she wished it to do; she would not have to always live within and under the transparent power she knew moved about her, over her, flattening her, pressing her, always pressing her like a huge continuous supersonic din.

There were very few cars on the highway and her mother drove as if she was bored. They were headed toward Napa, where they would have lunch in a gray Victorian house with a broad wooden porch. The wisteria would not be in its lavender and white bloom but still she liked sitting in the wicker chairs with the light filtered through the vines and leaves and the murmur of traffic far away. She looked forward to the cool light and the calm chime of dishes and silverware. She did not think about food or about appetite; she thought about how long it would take to get there and how long they would have to wait in the high, deep parlor with the heavy furniture, and about what her mother might have meant by saying, "Let's have lunch on your father."

Her mother twirled her hair in her fingers and Lisa knew she was getting ready to speak. Her mother kept glancing into the rearview mirror and every time she did a mote of light leapt across the glove compartment from the lens of her sunglasses. They were on a slight decline about to approach a steep hill.

"I wish that truck would get off my tail," her mother said.

She sat up and turned around. It was a huge truck with quilted tin siding and it followed so closely behind the Mercury that she could see the mud on the license plate.

"He wants to pick up momentum for this hill, but he can change lanes to do it," her mother said.

She kept her eyes on the truck. It seemed to be getting closer. She turned back around to see that the incline was just beginning. She could feel her mother braking the car gradually. The truck was having to back off. She read 40 mph on the speedometer, but it was continuing to go down. The truck driver's heavy arm pushed straight into the horn in the middle of the large steering wheel and the deep bellow resounded in the pit of her stomach. The Mercury's speedometer now read 25 mph and she could see the truck driver's arm move and then the truck chug and lurch desperately into a lower gear. The Mercury began to pick up speed and as the car crested the hill her mother laughed and turned to her with as beautiful a smile as she had ever seen. She looked back at the truck far below them; it was dark and mean-looking, crawling ever so slowly up the hill.

"So, your father has a girlfriend? One who wears expensive clothing."

"I don't know," she said, quietly surprised that her mother

didn't know about Mary, though she knew she'd never mentioned Mary for fear of hurting her mother's feelings.

"You don't know about the girlfriend or you don't know about the clothes?" her mother asked.

"Could we talk about something else? I don't know about her clothing."

"What's her name?"

"Her name?" she stammered. "What does it matter? I mean, why do you want to know? What difference does it make?"

She didn't want her mother to know anything, she wanted Mary and her mother as separate as she could keep them, unaware of each other, unhurt by each other.

"Elisabeth."

"Don't call me that. My name's Lisa."

"Your name is Elisabeth, in case you have forgotten, young lady."

"My name's Lisa. You all call me Lisa. Don't call me Elisabeth."

"What's wrong with the name Elisabeth? That's where your name derives from. Remember, you're named after me."

"Okay. Okay. I just want to be called Lisa."

"What's her name, Elisabeth?"

"No. Her name's not Elisabeth."

"Don't get smart. What's her name?"

"I just don't see why you need to know."

"What the hell is her name, Lisa?" Her mother slammed her hand into the steering wheel.

"It's Mary. Mary. Mary. Mary. Okay, are you satisfied? Mary, Mary, Mary."

"I just want to know who's been around my daughter. I have a right to know some things, Lisa. A right. You may understand that someday. You obviously don't understand it right now. Does she spend the night while you're there?"

"I don't know," she said. The mote of light flashed across

the glove compartment and stayed there for an instant. She felt the passage of air stopped in her throat, choking her.

"You're going to tell me you don't know who's there in the morning at the breakfast table?"

She could see the streets of Oakland on either side of the car. There were the tall poles of filling stations which made the different logos easy to see from the freeway, and the large stucco apartment complexes which still looked sodden from the California rain even though it had been a dry summer. The green freeway signs ticked past, 157th Street, 148th, 139th, and almost suddenly there were many more cars driving the lanes alongside the Mercury.

"Certainly he doesn't sneak her out before you get up, Lisa?"

"Yes, she spends the night—she lives there."

Now passing her eyes were warehouses with huge easeled billboards atop their brick structures and then the beautiful cement sweep of the freeway splitting off into another major freeway and continuing up and over the oncoming lanes.

"Doesn't seem to have many clothes, then. What's she like?" her mother asked, her hand reaching up near the window once again to twirl her hair between her fingers.

"She's nice," Lisa said. "Her name is Mary."

"Yes, I seem to remember hearing that repeated several times already."

She was trying to forget that she had screamed Mary's name. She just wanted to say Mary's name quietly, to say it the way it deserved to be said, quietly and with kindness. Her thoughts of Mary did not deserve to be forced into the tension of the car. Mary had been good to her, had taken her shopping for a good coat, which they had never found because she, Lisa, tended to be too particular. The selection had been either nylon parkas which surrounded one's body like a balloon or Empire-line coats with velvet collars which she thought beautifully formal but also somehow not right for Sonoma and its ruralness.

Yet she liked formality. There was something about it that assured one of consistency, of being treated with a certain agreed-upon etiquette. A maître d' would always be tall and white-haired, polite and with a gracious accent to his speech. And good clothes that were a touch formal always seemed to range a distance between you and others, a comfortable distance like enough time to make a dinner table perfect before guests arrived; they weren't knocking at the door before the flowers were on or the napkins folded into fans or lotus blossoms; people weren't pushing you aside as just a child, a stupid brat, before they knew you, or knew what you wanted of them.

She had liked a red coat with a velvet collar the color of mink. The velvet had felt like the tail of a Siamese cat she once played with on the floor, rolling a little cotton mouse around before its quick paws, watching its body dance in circles and its velvet tail sweep past her face and around her neck and across her eyes. But the red coat was expensive and perhaps not quite right, and if it was Mary who was paying for it, it would not have been polite to choose such an expensive article.

Perhaps she would have asked for it had she known that her father was paying, but it was Mary shopping with her and it was Mary's purse from which the money would be taken. She could not be sure and so she did not choose a coat that day but merely held the memory of the red one among her many desires as if it were a particularly favorite layer within a pastry she would someday eat alone and independent at a small table in a foreign land with the sunlight pouring in through the panes of an old European door so perfect and beautiful she could see its carved fruit and its crystal bevels before her as though she had actually seen this door many times and would pass through it many more.

"What does she do?"

"Something with plants."

"A florist. How quaint," her mother said with a high-pitched voice. Lisa shook her head. "What? A botanist?" her mother then said.

The Mercury veered away from the Bay Bridge and Lisa could see only the tip of San Francisco's skyline through the dense fog that hung over the bay.

"No. Or at least that's not what she calls it. She's a horti-culture—ist, or something like that."

"You can lead a horticulture but you can't make her think."

"What?"

"Dorothy Parker. Perhaps not exactly but pretty close."

"Oh."

"A writer."

"What's that mean, though?" she asked. "Can't make her think?"

"Nothing, Lisa. Nothing."

"You ask me questions. You make me give you answers. Why can't you just explain something to me? So what if I don't get it, can't you just tell me?" The tears swelled in her eyes; the road blurred before her. She was trying to figure it out, trying to be smart. Mary. Horticulture. Think, she kept saying to herself, think. It was "you can lead a horse to water but you can't make it think—drink"—that was it. But that wasn't the phrase. You can lead a horse to culture, horticulture, horse to culture, horticulture—and then she got it. "Mary is not a whore," she said angrily.

"It's just an expression, sweetheart. It really doesn't mean anything. Okay? Come on. Let's have a good day." Her moth-er's hand reached across and patted her on the leg. She let it rest there for several miles. "The roses are blooming like crazy at home and that damn fig tree just keeps putting out. I've frozen several containers of them. We'll have to come up with some way to use more figs."

"I don't like figs," she said in a whisper. "They're too sweet."

Elisabeth laughed. "I don't see how you can drink Coke and not think it too sweet and then call figs straight from the tree too sweet."

"Yeah, but they're like eating sand too. I hate those seeds they have." They were traveling without much traffic now. They passed the turnoffs for Vallejo and Benicia and continued on the freeway with the gold, dry hills on either side standing very still and bright beneath the blue sky.

"The last countryside in California," her mother said. This did not mean that much to her. She wanted a big city. She wanted San Francisco or perhaps Paris, though she had never been to Paris. She wanted the huge cocoon of namelessness which she was sure life among that many people granted you. Or perhaps it was not namelessness but independence, independence from the expectations people you knew had of your person and of what you said and of how you said it.

She was sure she could be another person in the city, a free person, a person who didn't have to depend on others for anything. She wouldn't be a burden. She could buy a red coat and take herself out to a quiet lunch with a good book.

The restaurant would have pink tablecloths and spindly chairs painted gold like the one she had seen a ballerina using as an impromptu barre in a painting by Degas. And there would be a rosy reflection from the tablecloths in the silver sugar bowl and vase. She would prop her book open with a small round plate and the vase's pink rose would cast a shadow down across the novel's creamy pages. In the lateness of the lunch hour she would sit alone in the restaurant, where tables were now being reset for the dinner service. She would not be bothered except occasionally by the waiter, who fussed very silently over her as though she were a precious water supporting some rare form of life that should not be disturbed.

The car slowed and began to list jerkily around the circular off-ramp into the calm, small-town streets of Napa.

"Shall we wait for lunch a bit? Do some junking first?" her mother asked.

She could feel her stomach hollowing out, but her mother seemed happy, excited even; lunch could wait forever as far as Lisa was concerned. Elisabeth pointed out a narrow, turreted Victorian house with a porch off the second story that was surrounded by a squat iron fence of points and curlicues.

"That's a widow's walk," her mother said. "Or rather, that's what they call a widow's walk."

"Did there used to be a lot of widows?" she asked.

"Did there used to be a lot of widows? Hmmm. I suppose that's an interesting question—did there used to be a lot of widows? A lot more than now?" The Mercury slowed at a light and Elisabeth rolled her window down and reached her arm out to click her nails against the side of the car. "Maybe so, because of the wars, but these were built long before that."

"I thought a lot of women used to die in childbed," she asked.

"Where'd you get that expression, 'childbed'?"

"I don't know. Read it, I guess. Why, what's wrong with it?"

"Nothing. It's just out of date."

"Like archaic."

"Yes, like archaic, smarty."

Elisabeth turned her head right and left searching the street for a parking place near the Women's League of Napa Thrift Store. Lisa breathed deeply as the car passed under a canopy of elms whose leaves were just beginning to turn the color of tarnished brass. She leaned forward into the windshield and looked up at the basket of branches and leaves shading them from the noon sun. I love this, she said to herself, this cool darkness the trees keep from the hot day outside. This must be how it is to die stretched out quietly in the dirt with your world fading steadily from your mind like parasites leaving flesh that has died and can no longer support them. She understood about dead flesh and live flesh, about how some parasites thrived on one and some on the other. Her father had told her about how hunters and soldiers would put maggots into their gangrenous wounds if they were not near doctors or a hospital and how the maggots ate only the decaying flesh and so would keep the wounds clean, would in fact keep the gangrene from spreading. But that was dead flesh, he had said, running the cleaning rod down the barrel of his gun, "and most parasites like the live stuff." He told her about people in the Middle Ages who were so vermin-infested that when they died and were laid in the cavernous stone churches, a small roar would go up as the lice and fleas scampered from their decaying bodies. It occurred to her that everything was an exchange, a compromise, a decomposition and a composition at once: death was at once a muteness and a roar, a gift and a sacrifice, a reality and a lack of everything which could possibly mean reality. Her hands were clutching the dashboard, and as she leaned toward the windshield she could smell her father's cologne, and when she stepped from the car across the leaf-laden gutter, she smelled the leaves and the cologne and the moist garden dirt in the flower beds being turned under in order to plant bulbs for the springtime.

"This place has a widow's walk too," she said, pointing toward the spearheaded iron rising up from the eaves of the house. "The widow who lived here had to go all the way to the roof."

"It was a vantage point," Elisabeth said. "She could look out over the town and the surrounding fields and see if her husband was coming home or not."

"I thought her husband was dead," she said, her voice obscured by the tinkling of a bell attached to the door of the old house. "I thought she was a widow."

"Lisa, it's architecture. Okay? I don't know whether she was or was not a widow. Right?" Her mother's fingers were brushing the bangs from her eyes. "Come on. Stop frowning, you'll have wrinkles before I do." Her mother's voice sounded like springtime, like hope, like narrow shoots of green rising through the moist darkness into the light. She watched her mother's lips push out and open into a smile like a blossom parting its petals to be born. They were going to have a good time, she thought. Their arguments would be forgotten. They were going to bury the past; the vermin would be the past and would crawl from them, would crawl from their deadening memories. The vermin might roar for a time, but then they would slowly become muter and muter till they no longer moved within the ground of their life together.

They were going to have a good time. Her father would not be thought of, and when the time came that he was thought of, she knew her mother would prey upon her, would eat at her until once again his memory, his time with her, his influence over her, was gone, excised, buried. She was trying to deaden that part of her which longed for her father, trying to let it fall from her heart and mind so that her mother would always be there running her fingers through her hair, smiling her beautiful smile. She was pushing him away as her foot could have pushed at the dead leaves in the gutter outside. She was turning him under and into the moist dirt and with him went the vermin and the maggots, all the parasites which ate away at her mother's happiness.

She was going to keep her mother happy. She saw her standing, leaning over a counter of jewelry. Two older ladies stood behind the counter and the three of them were laughing. Her mother was making them laugh as she could always make people laugh, telling them about "the Filthy Packers of London" who never had their clothing cleaned and so would pin silk roses over the spots on their clothing. "London society was scandalized—roses showed up in the strangest places." The women were giggling as they bent to retrieve different brooches and pins, and then the black silk rose which had started the story appeared on the glass as though it had sprung full-bloomed from the sparkle and glitter of the counter.

She passed her fingers through a rack of white lace petticoats and then hunched down before a shelf of books to read titles. Their faded bindings did not appeal to her love of books. She liked new books with immaculate covers and pages which did not smell of dust. Most of the books before her she had no idea about. They had authors and titles that alarmed her. Who were they? Should she read them? Would she be asked about them ever? Perhaps she could figure out which book was more important to have read by the price marked in pencil just inside the cover of each. She began to pull books from the shelf to inspect their prices. Blue covers, black ones, brownish ones, and always that waft from between the old pages like a dirt smell just before it begins to rain.

"Do you need some new books?" her mother asked, walking over to her. Lisa saw the black silk rose and a Pyrex leftover dish.

"No, I have some books still to read. They're in the car even," she continued, as if this were meaningful. She didn't mention that her father had given them to her, that they were Hemingway—"the world's most stupid writer," her mother had said once.

"Nothing here, then? Lunch?"

"Sure."

IN THE RESTAURANT, under the parlor's white marble mantel, where Lisa thought a small fire should have burned calmly, a huge vase of hydrangeas stood, their blossoms like the woolly heads of sheep. They were purplish blue and greenish white and she found them oddly colored for flowers.

"They're flowers which like a lot of nitrogen," her mother was saying. "Like rhododendrons and azaleas. That's how those purple and fuchsia tones come about. Nitrogen."

Her mother seemed to be talking to no one in particular and so Lisa thought of a woman in this parlor with kid-and-lace-clad feet sitting before the fire reading a book or needle-pointing a pastoral scene which would then be stretched tautly over chair or settee springs for upholstery. She would have been a tiny woman, she mused, not a woman as tall as her mother, and her hands would have worked the needle and canvas almost without looking.

She tried to picture who had worn the smooth depressions in the hardwood floor before the hearth. A man in shining boots and tight white pants who stood with his hands behind his back. She could see him there before the marble, his legs slightly apart and a manner of speaking from deep within his throat which created in the small woman doing needlepoint a slow cresting like waves that inspired her body. The woman's hands began to work the needle more quickly and with these stitches she kept her eyes on the pink roses just beginning to bloom from the canvas. The man regarded the woman's kid shoes and the tatted lace hem which reached well below the shoes' heels, which curved in and then out again like certain vases or balustrades. How could feet be so tiny? he would be thinking. Lisa imagined that he would be delighted with the fragility of the scene before him and that he would be careful, extremely careful, not to disturb this tranquillity. The room was quiet, no music, no engines or machines. A bird, she thought, perhaps a bird sang occasionally from the elm stand-ing before the house. But no, she preferred it quiet, completely silent. The room in all its whiteness, silent. A creak from the floorboards before the fireplace and yes, of course, the sound of a log tamping into ashes against the grate, but silence in and around these quiet sounds.

"Sandham." A woman in a knee-length dress called their name across the parlor. Her mother stood up; people were milling around; a child bounced up and down on a velvet-covered pouf before the bay window. "Sandham." She heard her name very distinctly this time. She rose from the carved chair and followed the figure of her mother. Her shoes, and others', against the wooden floor sounded clamorous—and why wasn't someone controlling that child bouncing on the furniture, she thought, and why were all these people here? The man she had imagined before the fireplace had just been about to say something. But now sound caromed within the room and the man with shining boots settled deeply into her mind as a sun at twilight is vibrant one moment and then gone. She looked back behind her to see a man with a yellow bow tie lowering himself into the carved chair where the woman with the needlepoint roses had been. She tucked her hand between her mother's elbow and waist as the hostess led them from the entry hall through the main dining room and out onto the porch.

The wicker chair sounded like a fire of dry twigs as she sat down in its woven lap. Brown canes of wisteria vine snaked along the eaves and followed down the columns of the porch. In places, wisteria crept through the ceiling boards and long, frondlike leaves made their way along the tongue and groove as though they were painted there the way the inside of a porcelain cup is often garlanded with leaves and tendrils.

"I'm hungry," she said, looking at her mother's blond hair brushed back from her face in one smooth wave. "I thought we'd never eat."

"I bet you weren't thinking about eating at all," Elisabeth said. "I bet you haven't thought about food for hours."

"I think about it," she said, laughing a bit. "Sometimes.

But I do like eating out because the water always tastes so good in restaurants. It never tastes like this at home."

Her mother smiled. "There's something true about that. The atmosphere, I suppose."

"No, I don't think it's that," she said. "It's the water. It's softer."

Ice chimed in the glasses and seemed to move in a dance with the sunlight shimmering through the frondlike leaves. The fire in the weave of the wicker chairs burned slowly, rasping from time to time. They ate cold salmon with pale yellow mayonnaise and tiny buns of bread baked with rosemary. She sipped at her mother's wine occasionally and felt the dull rise of its alcohol between her eyes and in the deep base of her forehead. She pulled a white needle of bone from her mouth and laid it alongside the foil butter wrapper on her bread plate. Her mother looked beautiful in the cool light with the creams and corals of their luncheon before her smooth complexion as though their lives were now coordinated perfectly with the world. Even the rim of gold around their luncheon plates seemed to rise up to match the gold of her mother's rings; even this seemed purposeful and elegant. It was that observable rightness that she loved. She sensed it was to be found in activities governed by formality and etiquette— and mostly in solitude and perhaps in that life she would lead once she was old enough, once she was free from this waiting to be old enough.

SHE HAD BEEN AWAY from Sonoma for two weeks. Little seemed changed as they drove down Broadway toward the town square, toward the stone courthouse directly before them, quaint and washed-out-looking. She felt welcomed by the familiarity of the shops and offices: there, the French bakery vestibule jammed with customers, and there, on the steps of the library, kids she knew from school, and over there, the law offices looking as locked and impenetrable as always.

They turned off the square down East Spain Street, driving past the mission and the old artist's house from whose lawn rose the rusted metal sculpture of a woman and her child furled together by a huge snake. Apples and their leaves sprang from the woman's hair and about her feet. She held a rust-pocked knife driven through the snake's body, and driven past, into her own throat. Lisa saw the woman as delighted, trium-phant even, her mouth lifted to the heavens with the blade driven deep into the darkness of her own interior. The child's metal arms were bound by the snake to the woman's pelvis and legs. Lisa hated the look of terror in the child's hollow eyes. Someday she would tell Mr. Kripke how wrong the child was. She didn't really care about the woman, about the knife or the snake, that was biblical, she thought, or mythological, whatever, but the child came off as naïve and clinging. Not all children were babies. She would walk up to Mr. Kripke and stand close to him so that she looked up into his thick gray beard as though she were under a tree hung with moss and say, You know that kid, Mr. Kripke, the one in the sculpture, well, it's wrong, it's clinging and stupid. Any kid she knew would fight and shout and try to get the snake off his mother. And even if the kid knew his mother was going to die because of the knife, she was convinced that wouldn't stop him from struggling. Sure, it was not very pleasant, the snake, but you didn't think about those things while they were happening. The mother would die no doubt, and maybe that was all the more reason for the child to fight harder against the snake, so that his mother wouldn't die thinking he was a stupid, useless kid.

She imagined Mr. Kripke on the lawn with his blowtorch forming the child's arms so that they were tensed and struck out at the thick coil of the serpent's body. Mr. Kripke would look through his mask at her to check the changes and she would motion to the child's eyes, that those too needed to be changed. She wanted them alert, sensible, hard even. What was in people's minds, she wondered, what did they think? That the child wanted to sit down and eat apples while the snake slithered about? Mr. Kripke would nod at her and move the torch's clear tongue across the child's face. In moments the eyes would be transformed, they would even burn red-hot for a while from the heat of the torch.

The Mercury was just then turning into their gravel drive. The line of cottonwoods stretched down the back road, tall and sedate. The field of wheat behind the house leaned in the breeze and every here and there a sunflower, its yellow-and-black face, looked out from the expanse of land.

"When did they bloom?" she asked. "They're crazy. How amazing."

"Oh. I suppose they started just after you left."

"It looks like leopard skins. Or just leopards. Hundreds of leopards all standing around in the field behind our house. I can't believe this."

"I've managed to sneak a few for the house. They take up a whole room, though."

"That color," she said. "I can't believe the color." She was excited, standing on the back porch looking out through the large windows. The sunflowers were like a welcome-home to her, like a party.

The house felt cool. Everything seemed neat and precise as she walked through the rooms. There were no dishes on the draining board. Nothing sat on the dining-room table, or on the staircase waiting for someone to take it upstairs. The umbrellas leaned in their wooden stand by the front door. The three settees around the fireplace in the living room were straight. She looked at their silent casters under the narrow curving legs. On the tiles before the fireplace a crock for pickling held several sunflowers and some branches of leaves. A book about painters during the time of Napoleon sat on the coffee table. It looked to her like no one had ever opened it, though she had spent hours gazing at the portraits by David and Ingres, their lines perfect, careful, a world in which intimacy was protected with unwavering reserve, a world of seclusion within the ease of very set proprieties. Elisabeth thought the paintings cold and distant.

She could hear her mother at the back of the house starting the hose to water. The house smelled fresh. There was no dust anywhere, nor any smell of food or perfume. Except for the sound of the water traveling through the pipes, there was complete silence and stillness.

There was something tremendously reassuring to her about the stillness, as though she could walk through these rooms and disturb nothing, as though she could travel here within this life and never leave any trace that she had lived. This was her mother's house, her mother's cool beauty, so precise and calm; she knew she was always fracturing it. But if she were careful no one would ever know she had been here, had even lived here. She could understand why certain people wanted to leave no trace of their life. She understood the burning of manuscripts and paintings, the demolition of houses and pieces of art. These were products of one life which burdened another. She wanted to be perfect grace, to bother no one, to pass through their lives gently as a breeze travels through curtains for a time and then releases them to hang straight and perfect once again. She could see from the straightness of everything that this was how her mother liked her house, that this was how she chose to live while she, Lisa, was away. Lisa vowed not to disturb it but rather to protect it as though it protected her mother and kept her happy.

"Lisa," her mother called from the back porch. "Lisa, come get your things, honey." The floor groaned loudly as she started to move from the living room. The sound shot through her feet and paralyzed her. She wanted to hide, to sink down behind a chair and curl into something infinitesimal, a sweet memory, an eventless day, a porcelain button sewn on a dress folded deep within a wooden trunk in a dark attic.

But she was not something infinitesimal; she had arms and legs and feet—and they walked—not without noise—through the passage to the kitchen and onto the porch.

Through the porch windows she could see her mother leaning over the flower boxes which lined the carport. Her mother held the hose with one hand and pulled at dead leaves and flowers with the other. The water gurgled through a perforated aluminum ball attached to the end of the hose. It clunked tonelessly against the wood of the planter boxes. Water darkened the concrete. She walked to her mother and put her arms around her from behind. The cotton felt cool and warm all at once. "I love you," she said. Her mother turned within her arms, the dress twisting around her tall body. Her mother's arms reached around her. The watering bulb fell from the planter to the concrete with a clatter. Water spewed around their shoes.

"I love you too, baby. I've missed you so much." Elisabeth stooped to retrieve the hose. She held Lisa's shoulder. "It's just never the same without you."

"Well, I'm back."

"You're back."

"Right." They were arm in arm, moving slowly along the flower boxes. There were red and yellow zinnias and spidery chrysanthemums.

"Are you really back?" Elisabeth asked, squeezing Lisa to her. "Really?"

"Of course I'm back, Mom," she said with a touch of exasperation. "What'd you think? I'm right here, aren't I?"

"Sure. You're my little girl. Right here."

"Mom. Come on. What's wrong? What'd you mean? Am I really—"

"You're so quiet when you come back. I wonder if you want to be back. I wonder if maybe you wouldn't rather be with your father."

"I want to be here. I'm really happy to be home."

"You consider this home?"

"Of course this is home," she said as her mother walked to the faucet to turn it off. The round handle squeaked as she turned it. Lisa could see that she looked as if she was about to cry. "Mom. Please." The aluminum watering bulb scraped across the concrete as Elisabeth mounded the green hose into coils at the base of the faucet.

"You don't hate me for taking you away from your father?"

It had never occurred to her to hate either of them. Hate. The idea seemed preposterous and then menacingly possible. It was like a fear of something you're not afraid of until someone mentions it, and then it's there, strong and nagging and exhausting.

As the aluminum bulb came to settle on top of the neatly coiled hose, she remembered the house in Castro Valley emptied of furniture, and the dust roiled up by the movers' work boots settling on the hardwood floors her father had sanded and varnished till they shone. She remembered the moving truck parked carefully under the sparse eucalyptus trees so that perhaps the trees would obscure a view of the truck from the sky should her father happen to fly by. She knew it had all been planned. The movers knocked on the door and asked if the truck's position seemed good enough to Elisabeth—they knew they were clearing a house of furniture and belongings while a husband worked through the day anticipating his return that night, as he had returned every night for years, to his home and his family; it had been planned. And yes, she had felt something driving to Sonoma with her mother several years before, the vision of their empty house in her head like shame.

She had not felt hatred for either of her parents, though. That emotion had only now presented itself, and yet, as an alternative to the responsibility she felt for what had happened, and for her shame and guilt, it seemed paltry, hollow, a cowardly child's way out. She didn't feel she could blame or hate anyone else for something she had not been brave enough to stop or make better. She could not hate her mother; in fact, she hadn't ever really considered her mother's responsibility at all. Her mother had been at the helm, yes, but then there had seemed something absolute about that, as though her mother were only carrying out a type of destiny; it was she, Lisa, who had been responsible, because she had stood by and done nothing.

"I don't hate you; you're my mother." She could see dark sprinkles of water on her mother's dress. "How could I hate you?" Her mother looked at her across the concrete. Her eyes were a deep, somber blue. "Mom," she said. "Hey, I'll even eat figs to make you believe me."

She could see her mother's mouth turning upward, some of the tension falling from it, but then she heard the quick squeak of a laugh being swallowed in tears and she knew her mother was crying.

"Are you all right, Mom?" She put her arms around her mother's waist. "Mom?"

"Just doubt; always doubt." They walked onto the back porch together. "Hey," her mother said, pointing to her luggage. "You haven't got these upstairs yet."

She watched her mother wipe her eyes roughly and then twist her hands together, rubbing the moisture into them as though she were rubbing in lotion. Her mother seemed unreachable, the way a baby in a hospital nursery is unreachable across the clear distance of glass and linoleum and space.

"What do children do with all the time they have from not doing what they're told?"

"I'm not a kid anymore, Mom."

"You're not? Oh."

"Now you're laughing? I'm not a kid."

"Oh."

"Mother, you better stop this."

"Well, I was just wondering what you are if you're not my kid."

"I am *your* kid. I'm just not *a* kid."

"Oh. Well, you've got that figured out. You're just an honorary member, right?"

"Okay, okay. I'm going upstairs."

Her bedroom door stood ajar. She pushed her bag against it to open it further. The door flew back quickly and she reached out to grab it before it knocked against the back wall. She loved the way the house tilted, how her closet door always swung wide if she wasn't careful to close it tightly, how marbles rolled down the room, under her bed, and pinged against the baseboards of the opposite wall. She loved having to chase the bedroom door in order to prevent it from banging into the wall; it was like a contest with a very silent, grand opponent who was just a bit mischievous; in this moment, she felt delighted to be home.

And in the next moment too she felt delight as she saw on her bed several packages, and the walls covered with green frogs and orange birds of paradise, red lobsters and pink and gray elephants—dozens of little origami animals with notes written on them in her mother's tall hand: "May pink elephants always flap their ears over you when you're hot"; "May your life's frogs always be princes"; "From one bird to another in a paradise of their own making," and many more notes which told her how much she had been missed a certain day or what food her mother hadn't made because it reminded her too much of their meals together. Everywhere she looked, super-imposed on lampshades and desk legs, on bedposts and drawer pulls, were paper animals, and here and there, a package wrapped in white paper sat with yet another bright animal decorating its stark surface. She set her book bag down and went back out without touching anything. She dragged her suitcase into the room and then went downstairs, where she found her mother in the kitchen setting a tray with iced tea.

"You go get some mint and we'll have a party in your room, if I'm invited?"

"Thanks, Mom."

"I was bored, so I took up the art of paper folding. Very inscrutable art, that. Don't look too closely at some of those attempts. That goddamn lobster was the worst."

"Thank you."

"Well, the operative word now is 'mint': take the scissors."

"Would you teach me how to fold some of them?"

"Forget it. Mint."

"Come on."

"I never want to see a piece of origami again in my life. I'm practically blind."

"Just the easiest animal, then. A bird."

"So, you think birds are easy. Ingrate."

"Where's the mint?" she asked, clattering the scissors across the tile of the countertop.

"What do you mean, where's the mint? You know as well as I do where the mint is."

"An elephant, then?" she said, opening and closing the blades of the scissors, the sound to her like the paper cutter at school, that quick, authoritative slicing that put her nerves on edge.

"Elephants are pretty easy. That I must admit. You might even notice a certain proliferation of them for that very reason."

"So, you'll teach me how to fold an elephant?"

"Will you eat figs for it?"

"That's not fair."

"Would you consider getting some mint in exchange for an elephant?"

She looked her mother in the eye with the confidence of a sure bluff in a fast game of poker. "An elephant and a frog."

"Why don't you recheck the book out of the library and teach yourself?" Her mother was loading ice-cube trays into the freezer.

"Will you help me?"

"Knowing you, you'll help me."

"That's not true."

"It's very true," her mother said. "And anyway, look at this." She pointed at the glasses of ice tea. "Stick with me, kid, and you'll have ice cubes as big as diamonds. Please, please, go get some mint."

SHE PULLED THE BEDSPREAD down and sat with the pillow between her back and the headboard. Her mother sat in the desk chair with her feet propped on the bed rails. The white eyelet spread hung down over her bare feet. The tea tray sat on the nightstand in front of the porcelain lamp. Lisa gathered the top of the bedspread and made a ridge with it between her feet and the little stacks of packages on the rest of the bed. "I love surprises," she said.

The sun was getting low and cast a dim pattern from the lace curtains across the floorboards. She thought for a moment about light, about what it was and why it seemed always to be of a pattern in her life, wrought iron or leaded panes or lace. She thought light was not something uncontained, diffuse, so much as it was the shadow of that which it shone through.

She liked the time of day nearing twilight because she could always see the darkened outline of things emerging. Light isolated itself, sank down below the bureau, and disappeared, coming up as different moons wherever she turned a switch or lit a candle, or coming up outside as the moon itself. Daytime was not a good time to see things, to see the crevices, the crannies and nooks. Daylight was too obscuring a type of light; surfaces were more what they were when the slow dimness rubbed across them as one can run a pencil over hieroglyphs bringing up onto the paper a sterner, deeper image.

She could see the half-light just beginning to outline the jars of beads on her worktable and the tiny pairs of manicure scissors standing in a cardboard box she had covered with paisley paper. She could see her dressing table scattered with small boxes of porcelain and wood, boxes collected for her for as long as she could remember, boxes given her on birthdays and holidays and as gifts brought to her from other people's trips. "Your time will come," her mother always said when she opened their tiny lids to see if ever there was anything inside. "Your time will come."

Now, spread before her across the bed were tiny white packages, some with bright animals and some left unadorned. She shook a few back and forth; she didn't know what she was hoping for and the contents rattled dully in their cardboard without her really paying much attention. They were school supplies, or barrettes perhaps. She was forever being sent back upstairs to clip her hair behind her ears or off her forehead. It didn't matter to her what was in her birthday packages; she didn't like surprises and she was puzzled about saying just the opposite moments earlier. There had been surprises and she felt tired of them.

"Before I forget," her mother started. "You should write a thank-you note to your father's—to Mary. You're obviously fond of her and it would only be right."

She had written letters to Mary over the years, written them at school in the library, folded them and sank them deep into

her biology book or her math text, where they stayed for a
day until she got a stamp from the post office after school and
an envelope from home that evening.

"Lisa. Do you hear?"

"Sure. Yes, I'll do it. But I already left a note for her at the
house."

"Oh. Well, in that case—" Her mother looked distracted,
sort of angry, she thought, but sort of hurt too. Lisa felt
returned to the bad feeling of the argument they had had in
the car earlier. She thought they had left that all behind them,
that they could forget Mary and her father and the anger it
caused her mother, but here it was again. And now her mother
was asking that she write Mary and thank her. She wanted
each person in her life to be a separate entity entirely from
everyone else. She wanted them all in completely separate
worlds instead of the gnashing gears they all seemed to be.

For years she had not told her father anything about her
life with her mother, and likewise had not told her mother
anything of her visits to her father; she had learned that if she
mixed the worlds, there were ramifications, fights and subtle
but obvious remarks intended to damn one parent or the other:
the way her mother laughed too loud at jokes or her father's
"inability to perceive another human being's needs." She had
been amazed one day to hear herself lying instead of telling
her mother that her father had flown Mary and her to Lake
Tahoe for a weekend. Any treat like that meant a long dis-
cussion on money, how much her father had and just how
little in fact he was offering his own daughter by flying her to
Tahoe. "He damn well should fly you somewhere" would be
her mother's comment. And to tell her father about a day
spent with her mother roaming the antique shops brought a
barrage of sarcastic remarks that made her want to rear up
and defend her mother. Yet somehow her mother always found
out about the special trip and then grilled her about it as

though she, Lisa, had kept vital information from her. And if she talked to Mary, and she wanted to, she was sure everything she said went back to her father—though there had never been any evidence of that other than that after she talked to Mary he was gentler for a time. Only David seemed different in this respect. He seemed to hold her words to himself, to watch her reactions, to weigh them as though they figured in the sum being added up around her from day to day.

"How's David?" she asked, her voice sounding quick and tense. "I was just wondering. I mean, is it good that he's back from Arabia?"

"It's better to have you back, that's what. Now open some of these. You don't know this, but we have dinner plans for tonight, birthday dinner plans." Her mother reached for a package about the size of a bar of soap. The paper foot of a large green frog was Scotch-taped to the box's middle so that the frog looked as though it sprang from the small white surface. "Here. This one."

"Great frog."

"That's just a fun gift, nothing special."

" 'But my time will come' is what you're going to say, right? That's what you always say."

"That's what I always know. Here, this one too. Come on."

"I know I shouldn't ask, but do you ever miss Dad?" She wasn't sure why she was asking her mother this question; it had something to do with David and with her, Lisa, and with the way her mother insisted on knowing about Mary. She wanted her mother either to love David or to love her father. It seemed to her that once she knew this, she could relax.

"No, you shouldn't ask—"

"But—"

"Perhaps if this room didn't reek of his cologne you wouldn't be thinking about him, or about me and him."

"Oh. That'll go away." She held up a package whose wrapping seemed a bit looser than the others. "You didn't wrap this one, did you?" She didn't want her mother to start looking for the cologne. "I can always tell. You fold the edges in."

"David is coming for dinner tonight—" Her mother's face was cast in shadow, her hair no longer blond but ashen.

"He wrapped this, right?"

"Why is that smell so strong?" The room rested dimly around them. Lisa felt as though they sat within the hull of a thick squash and that the question hung over them like a moist thready membrane.

"What are you going to make for dinner?" She pulled the paper from the loosely wrapped package; the contents thudded in the box.

"That's from David."

"I know. Weren't you going to tell me?"

"I didn't want him to give it to you in the first place." She lifted a heavy chrome razor from the box. "When you start that, you'll have to do it for the rest of your life."

Once at the Sebastiani Theater she had heard a boy whisper in his girlfriend's ear that once the girl had sex she would want it always; to Lisa, shaving her legs seemed to fall into that category of things a girl would always want to do.

"It just doesn't seem like such a big deal," she said. "And anyway, you don't have to shave your legs when you're old."

"That's when you really have to because your body's going apeshit."

"Oh."

"What? Did your father douse you in cologne this morning? You smell like you've been rolled in it."

"It'll go away."

"Well, just so you don't—"

"Mom?" she began, her fingernail slicing through a band of Scotch tape. "Dad asked me to come live with him next year."

"So David told me."

"I just thought you should know."

"I don't really need to know about your father's fantasies, sweetheart."

SHE HUNG ON A BRANCH of the fig tree behind the house gazing at the dark disks of sunflowers in the field of wheat. She thought about what Mary would say if she saw them, some Latin name which would sound a bit staid for the silly flowers with their bright yellow petals, a name that would perhaps sound right for them as they were now, in the dark. She turned and looked at David's car in the lights from the back-porch windows. She wanted to learn to drive the Alpine because it looked like a little animal that she could get inside and be alone in and look out from as though she were in a costume. She wanted to drive it up the coast, passing through small, wood-frame towns suspended in fog and mist. She would be this tiny animal scampering beside the bluffs of tall grasses, this tiny red mechanical mole with bright round eyes and scurrying wheels like fast little paws in a hamster-cage hoop.

The carport lights switched on. "I need to go to my mother's for a second. Coming?" David stood beside her. He looked crisp, she thought, all camel and blue, the sand and water of a beach on a bright winter day, crisp, uncomplicated, the calm blue water his chest and the long, smooth sweep of beach his legs—and only once the brief rise of a dune like a gibbous moon beneath gabardine. Girls, women, didn't look this way: a hairdo or earrings or even the ribs of a brassiere showing obliquely through.

"What are we going to your mother's for?" she asked, dropping her hand from the fig branch.

"A recipe. For marinade." He swung the passenger door of the little red car open and motioned her in.

"Couldn't we just telephone?" She got into the car and David pushed the lock button down as he closed the door. The car smelled of rattan from the shredded mats on the floor. She heard his shoes on the gravel as he walked around to the driver's side and got in.

"I have a couple of other things to talk to her about—maybe even to you about."

"Couldn't we walk, then?" she said.

"I thought you liked this car."

"I do." She wasn't sure why she had suggested walking but the cool dimness of the evening seemed to call for a casualness, an ease, a conversation offered along the streets just beginning to mutter with the sound of fall leaves. "I don't know. It's just that—"

"We'll walk if you really want to walk." He was holding the keys against the steering wheel and she began to laugh. "What are you laughing at, silly?" he asked.

"Thanks for the razor. I think you made Mom mad."

"Jesus! Are we driving or walking? The way you and your mother change subjects."

"Can I drive?" she asked, but realized he wasn't listening.

"That razor was given to me by my father. I couldn't even shave when he gave the thing to me."

"I like the chrome."

"German chrome. The best made, and heavy. The thing feels good in your hand."

"Thank you, David. Maybe you shouldn't have given it to me."

"Your mother will get over it. You want to shave your legs—hell, shave your legs."

"No, I don't mean that. Your father gave it to you. Maybe you should keep it. It means a lot to you. I can tell."

"That's why I'm giving it to you. Just don't soak the thing in the tub. Take care of it."

"You don't have to worry. I will."

"I know you will, Elisabeth," he said, resettling himself in the car seat.

"Why is everyone trying to call me Elisabeth today? My name's Lisa."

"I was just trying it out."

"Why can't people just—"

"It's Elisabeth, though, really, isn't it?"

"If I want to be called Maggot, then people should call me Maggot. All of a sudden, I'm having to fight to have people call me by my name. What's the problem?"

"I was just running Elisabeth around in my mind, seeing how it fit. There's no problem. Lisa."

"Can I drive, then?"

"First I give you a razor against your mother's wishes, then I let you drive a car. She'll put me in the marinade."

"Chicken," she called him as he turned the car from the driveway down Spain Street.

"I am a chicken. That's right. If something happened to you, your mother wouldn't even want to live." The turn indicators clicked loudly as he waited for a car to pass before turning onto the street which led to his mother's. "Did you ever watch anyone drive a manual stick shift? Because probably the best way to learn is to watch someone else's feet. It's coordination."

"Well, it can't be impossible. A lot of people know how to do it."

"A lot of people do a lot of things they don't do well. There's such a thing as riding the brakes or riding the clutch or grinding the gears. Here, watch my feet."

"I can't really see that well. What's grinding the gears?"

"That would be like arguing with your mother."

"Very funny. Come on, what is it?" She held the thin cold bar of the door handle, about to get out in front of the white

Victorian house where Mrs. Armstrong lived alone with two American Standard poodles the color of conch shells.

"As I said, it's all coordination: the clutch, the gas, the gears. You flub one and all the rest make rather a horrible sound."

"You mean gnashing gears, not grinding."

"Gnashing—grinding—whatever."

"I thought they might be different. But then you wouldn't tell me if they were—no one ever tells me anything straight out."

"You're too much fun to tease," he said, getting out of the car.

What looked like the decorative hilt of a skeleton key extended out from a brass plate at the side of the tall double doors. David wound the handle and the bell thunked once and then twice before he reached for the wobbly doorknob. It rattled as he twisted it. He shooed her before him into the wide-open hall laid with wide, battered planks of oak and dotted here and there by thin, frayed rugs of such intricacy that she thought only to sit upon them and trace her finger in and around and through their arabesqueness as though her finger could make of her body a leaf falling in great turns and twists of wind. But suddenly the hall filled with the chatter of paws on wood and George and Martha muzzled a snout into each of her arms. She was in a whirl, the damp coolness of the dogs' noses, their affectionately urgent whimperings, the curly ears like wigs on English barristers, goofy but winsome and somehow emerging from that combination as sweetly grand. They pranced, their paws moving up and down like counterpoint tapped out on a windowpane, and their huge brown eyes looked like fine river stones, still and earnest and smooth. She leaned down onto her knees and wrapped her arms around their woolly necks, her face sandwiched between their ears, and gently pushed their backsides till they lowered their haunches and sat looking at her with patient excitement, as though she were everything in the world a dog could ever want.

"Mother," David called.

"Oh, you're such good dogs. Yes. Oh." She rose to her feet as Mrs. Armstrong came down the staircase. She wore a slim gray skirt, a white patterned blouse, and her white hair pulled back and furled into a French twist rose behind her just enough so that she looked regal and composed.

"I've figured out why your bank doesn't work, dear," she said to David, though Lisa could feel the woman's eyes on her. "It's the plants and flowers; you designed a stark, space-ship type of interior and all the tellers and secretaries have their philodendrons drooping all about making the thing look like Lillie Langtry's parlor."

"So next time I'll insist on clutter control," he said in a low voice. "Thanks, Mother," he said more audibly. "You know Lisa."

"I was admiring her cheekbones. Where did you get those, dear?"

Mrs. Armstrong always scared her a little. It was that type of scared one felt on being chosen for a really good team, that feeling of pride in being picked combined with fear that one wasn't good enough to keep company with the rest. She smiled and raised her shoulders; she didn't even know she had cheek-bones, or ones of note.

"So, I get to come to dinner tonight too. Well, I'm delighted. What recipe is it you wanted? Ida's marinade?"

"That's the one," David said.

"You're coming to dinner tonight?" Lisa asked, excited by the promise of hearing Mrs. Armstrong's precise voice speak through the evening, and then scared again. "Why didn't anyone tell me?" She was trying to smile again. Martha pushed her against a wall, wanting to be petted.

"They were afraid you'd veto the guest list, I suppose," Mrs. Armstrong said, her tall back now to Lisa as she walked across the living room to the narrow paneled doors which led through the dining room and into the kitchen.

"Your mother just invited her over the phone when we called for the recipe. Okay?" David leaned down to her ear and whispered, "Okay?"

"No, I'm happy," she said. "I like your mother." David smiled and then turned to take the stairs two at a time.

"I'll be right down."

"Who's Ida?" she asked, her face lifted up the stairs.

"Ask her at dinner."

She knew Mrs. Armstrong's house because one day years ago when she came with David to pick up some mail he had let her wander the house while he made phone calls from the study upstairs. She had walked slowly, the slightest creak or groan making her stop, frozen, to listen for Mrs. Armstrong's step through the rooms. To Lisa it felt as though she were snooping, walking around someone else's house with no particular purpose in mind. She had walked through the living room and found hanging from the dining-room ceiling a chandelier of blown-glass faces and, fascinated by this, had pulled a chair from under the table and sat down beneath the gallery of shiny black and white faces with dots of red glass for eyes and mouths and coils of brown or yellow glass for hair. She had thought too that sitting quietly at the long table looked the least suspicious should Mrs. Armstrong return and find her there without David. She had gotten up to turn the rheostat on the wall and had supposed that if she complimented her on the chandelier enough when Mrs. Armstrong came home, the older woman would not mind her having brought the light on in the transparent faces. But the rheostat illuminated the wall sconces and only then had Lisa realized that candles stood behind the little glass heads. She had felt silly for not noticing this before and quickly turned the sconces off, settling herself back down in the chair. She remembered commanding herself to carefully inspect everything in the room, every surface and detail, so that she would not miss anything, would not seem always to be missing the obvious.

Now she stood in the hall with George and Martha at either side of her. She didn't know whether to follow Mrs. Armstrong to the kitchen or to just wait, but then David came down the stairs and stood beside her, tearing open envelopes, the ripping noise shrill in her ears, an alien sound in the great, tall coolness of this house.

"How are we going to fit three people in your car?" she asked, thinking that perhaps David would stop tearing open his mail. His face tilted down toward an envelope whose sides he held apart, his eyes concentrating on the print or figures inside, and then he looked up at her as though he'd forgotten she was there.

"I'm sorry. What did you say?"

"Your car. It's not big enough for all of us."

"Jesus. You worry about everything," he said, his eyes directed back toward the envelope. "Mother will take her own car. Not to worry."

THE BRASS CANDLESTICKS stood high over the table and the candlelight moved like the slow twitches of moth wings. The chicken tasted of lime and ginger, and the yellow squash on the plates looked to her like mounds of gold coins.

"When I lived in San Francisco," Mrs. Armstrong was saying, "I had an Indonesian man who worked for me who came from somewhere near Djakarta. He used to say we had no idea what really good coffee tasted like." She threw her arms up in the air as if to say, Who knows? "Anyway, he was born to a fairly prosperous family, rich really, his father had tin mines, and he was one of a set of twins. There had been a sister delivered stillborn. Ida was told all this by a nurse, an amah, who had been hired to take care of him because his mother had rejected him at birth.

"His mother refused to breast-feed him because she said he had eaten enough inside the womb for two babies and that his life would obviously be a life of complete greed and she refused to nurture it in any way. If he had done what he did inside the womb, there was no telling what he was capable of in the world. She called him a *butas*, or a demon, and there was something about the Islamic idea of will but I don't know. As I remember, both sets of grandparents lived in the house, in several different wings, it was big, and Ida lived with his grandmother, his mother's mother, and the amah."

Lisa watched David's long arm reach across the table to pour wine for his mother. The wine caught a yellow light as it curled into the bowl of the glass. His mother did not stop her story but dipped her head and continued.

"Ida was very dark, too dark, his mother thought. She thought he looked very much like the shadow puppets her countrymen made of the devil, his long crooked nose and the blackish-red face. He was very swarthy to be sure, and much darker than his older brother, whom I met once, but certainly he wasn't darker than many an Indonesian. Anyway, one day his mother came into his grandparents' quarters, where he was playing. He told me he was seven at the time, and she made him undress completely and go out with her to a pond they had in the garden. There she had waiting a bucket with several scrub brushes, some of reed and some of wire that the servants used for cleaning the cement floor in the kitchen. She proceeded to try to scrub his skin into a lighter shade, and when the reed brushes didn't work, she began with the wire brushes. Ida used to laugh and say, Well, it worked, all his scars were whiter than the skin of anyone in his entire family."

She stopped to cut a piece of a chicken breast and push it onto the back of her fork. Lisa watched her slide the fork into her mouth and pull it out again. There was no hurry in her eating, no sign that hunger had ever urged her.

"Ida's face and hands were all I ever saw. That was enough. I'm sure his entire body looked the same way, like ridges in sand, or strips, striations I guess would be the word. Anyway, not good. But—and this I think should be a play or something—he went back home after the hospital. Well, he had to, I guess, he was only seven, but maybe he was older. Anyway, he decided that he would make himself into his sister, whom he had killed by his greed inside the womb. He insisted his grandmother have girl's clothing made for him—kains or sarongs—and he insisted that she teach him how to sew and cook, and how to dance. Ida told me he was grateful for the clothes because they covered him almost entirely. They were Muslims. This went on till he was about ten or eleven and was shipped to the United States to work for his uncle in a restaurant. His mother then began to write to him as though he were the dead sister, and did so until she died some years later when he already worked for me. I remember the envelopes, thin, airmail-type onionskin, but several sheets' worth of letter, and the large stamps. Beautiful stamps. When the letters came he would go into his room and dress in traditional dress and sit and read the letters, pretending he was his sister. And he wrote back. Wrote back as his dead sister—smoking those damn clove cigarettes the whole time, I might add.

"He told me that once he wrote to his mother as himself and said the sister was doing very well in America, that she was big and fat and happy, eating all the time, and that she missed her mother and her twin brother. The mother wrote back asking the sister what brother she referred to, that there was no twin brother, that indeed she had been born with a dark caul like a mask but that there had been no twin—no brother. 'I am a mask,' Ida would say to me when we worked together in the kitchen, 'a dark caul that my mother tried to scrub from her life.' "

"Could you tell me what a caul is, Mrs. Armstrong?" Lisa crossed her arms low in her lap and leaned her upper arms against the table. Outside a car passed on the street and as she looked from the window she saw David and her mother exchange glances.

"A caul, my dear," Mrs. Armstrong said, "is something some children are born with and some aren't. It's really just a membrane that covers a baby's head. Some cultures exalt it, others, including our own, couldn't really give a damn about it. Oh, sometimes people think of it as portentous, the child will be great or magical or something—"

"I bet you were born with one," David said to her, his head turning in his palm as he raked his hair from his forehead with his fingers.

"Was I?" she asked. Her mother coughed into her napkin as she pushed away from the table. "Mom?"

"What a thing to put into her head, David," Mrs. Armstrong said, looking at her son.

"Your story's charming too, Mother."

The room was silent for a moment and she fell back against the wooden splat of the chair. "Are you going to tell me? I deserve to know, don't I?"

"Well, you weren't born with a twin, that's for sure," Elisabeth said, laughing.

"I could have been born with both."

"You weren't."

"Was I born with a cowl?"

"Caul. Not that I remember," her mother said.

"But you would remember something like that, wouldn't you?" she asked, turning first to Mrs. Armstrong and then back to her mother.

"Ida's mother made it up, sweetheart," Elisabeth said.

"Ida's mother had twins, one died, one didn't—Ida. His mother made reference to him only as a caul, but he wasn't, he was in fact another baby, another child—not a membrane."

"I was listening. I know. But was I or wasn't I born with a caul?"

"That's called tenacity," Mrs. Armstrong said.

"All babies are born with membranes around them," Elisabeth said, resting her elbow across the chair back, her fingers reaching for a lock of hair to twist. "All babies have cauls."

"Oh." She sat silently for an instant and then bolted up against the table. "No they don't. How can they? Why would people talk about cauls if all babies had them—I mean talk about them as though they were special?"

Mrs. Armstrong laid her fork alongside her knife and said, "And she won't fall for that 'all babies are special' crap either."

"What if I said I was out like a light when you were born and I wouldn't know if you had a caul or not? Would that satisfy your monster curiosity? You know, these days if you don't have your baby naturally it's as if you aren't really a mother."

"Would Dad know?"

"Then you'd know whether you could drown or not," David said. "Isn't that the wives' tale? You'll never drown if you're born with a caul?"

"That's good, because I'm not a great swimmer."

"Lisa, you're a perfectly good swimmer, and you are not going to drown," her mother said.

"Would Dad know, Mom? About the caul?"

"I think we'll just have this little conversation later."

She held the words she was about to speak in her throat. She knew an expression was on her face that went with the words. David looked at her and she felt embarrassed as though he had caught her rehearsing for a play she had not gotten a part in.

"Louise, this recipe is from Ida?" Elisabeth asked, pointing to the platter of chicken pieces with slices of lime half congealed in pale sauce.

"Yes. He left me with many recipes. One in which the chicken is boiled in coconut milk. Wonderful. *Opor ajam*. I'll make that for you and Lisa sometime, with *gado gado*."

"God no, not the dread *gado gado*," David said.

"What is it?" Elisabeth asked, laughing, turning to Mrs. Armstrong.

"Hardly dread. It's a wonderful vegetable salad with peanuts. But my boy here does not like peanuts, so no one else is allowed either."

"Mother wishes to finish her story."

"Is Ida coming back?" Lisa asked.

"He may. But there's more. One evening, late, we'd had a party, he said to me, Dalang—he called me Dalang—I'll tell you later what that means. Dalang, I'm going back to Java to learn how to make shadow puppets, to learn Wayang. I have grown up a *butas*. Who better to make demon puppets? I have been a shadow—mask—demon—caul—all the makings of a puppet, but I am going to become my own puppeteer. All my life I have been what my mother thought me and then what my mother wished me to be, my dead sister. I suppose that if I can make the demon, a huge fat demon, then he will live outside me, away from me. I will be able to hang him on a hook at night, to look at him in the semi-darkness of morning and say, '*Butas*, you have slept there all night, not here, and you will not move till I take you from your hook, you will not move through anyone's life till I let you. Dalang—I will be my own Dalang.'

"So, you have called me a puppeteer these last few years, I said to him. You have called me what you would have called your mother, what you thought your mother was."

"What did he say then?" she asked.

"No, Dalang, he said, that is not it. Yes, at first I was angry

with you for permitting the letters to find me. I thought when
I left my uncle that no one could get to me, that I could stop
being my dead sister. But then when you came bringing that
stack of letters and I had to sit in my room and read them,
yes, then I thought of you as my Dalang. But you weren't,
were you? No, I was my Dalang. We are first puppets and
then we learn to be puppeteers, and what is inside us will
always cast shadows and what we make outside ourselves are
those shadows once again."

"And this is all while they're cleaning *gado gado* bowls,"
David said.

"Do you miss Ida, Louise?" Elisabeth asked. She dropped
her arm from the back of the chair and pulled her body back
to the table. She ran an index finger up and down the stem
of her wineglass. Lisa saw that the glass was empty and clouded
with smudges.

"Yes, very much," Mrs. Armstrong began. "But it always
strikes me as a bit resentful to miss people. They're off in their
own lives, and shouldn't they be?"

"What happens when someone dies?" Lisa asked. "Do you
miss them then?"

"She's rather uncanny, isn't she?" Mrs. Armstrong said.

"Except we don't talk about her in the third person because
it makes her angry," David said. "She'll start reading us all
with her silent, penetrating eyes."

"Stop it. I will not."

She cleared the dinner plates, lifting them carefully from
each place, making sure the silverware didn't slide off as the
rounded knife handles rocked gently back and forth on the
china. She took two plates at a time to the kitchen and then
returned. David tamped a pouch of tobacco on the tablecloth
and three tiny shreds of tobacco appeared near his coffee spoon
as she raised his plate from in front of him.

"So, you smoke a pipe now?" his mother asked.

"The British influence in Saudi, I suppose."

He lifted his pipe to his mouth and then slid his index finger and thumb down the narrow stem to its bowl; it was all one motion and Lisa felt awed by this smooth admission of one surface into another; it was sensual and clandestine and public. She watched the match he held between his fingers flare shortly in the candle flame and then settle as it traveled down toward the pipe's bowl, whose well as it took light became a network of minuscule neon worms.

She inhaled the smoke deeply. She could feel it filling her head, thick and white, but the aroma made her think of cherry-wood, the red-brown burnished surface, and then of the dry brown bark of twigs, those twigs so long ago that she had imagined in the Canadian tundra, the twigs that the moose was falling into, the moose whose antlers shed velvet as though a woman had flung her clothes over them, and then she thought of the aroma of coffee beans and of cocoa beans which she had smelled roasting at the chocolate factory in San Francisco, the huge metal drums like clothes dryers tumbling the waves of beans over the last wave of beans in a continuous cresting and breaking of oiled brownness. The smoke of the tobacco fogged the mottled light of the dining room. She looked at the cloudy smudges on the wineglasses and at the room filling in with tobacco smoke. She smelled that deep, rich pervasiveness that was masculine and foreign in this house. It was a smell which she felt pull something from the inside of her outward. It made her fill her lungs, awakening from her a chesty desire she did not think to name.

"Are you going to play that concerto for us?" David asked Elisabeth. He pulled the pipe from his lips. "The somber one."

From her mother's bedroom, she had brought the cello downstairs herself, lifting it from the gentle suction of the case's yellow interior, her fingers grasping the thin, stringed neck, the cello's buoyant lightness always surprising to her. She pictured the cello leaning now in a corner of the living room, its scroll turned toward the sunflowers in the fireplace as though it were a type of insect head surveying a possible source of food. She sensed of herself how foreign it was to be thinking of the cello, its tightly furled crest, its amber physique. She thought most often of the black case: how her mother's arm wrapped around its dark convexity when she carried it anywhere; how it rode in the front seat of the car next to her mother in her own seat; how she remembered it standing that first night in this house, at once a dark presence and an even darker absence; and how, through the years of her childhood, the case had remained in her eye and in her mind a black, featureless personage.

She turned her head as she went into the kitchen carrying the last dishes. Her mother was smiling carefully, her face tilted down; it was unusual for her to play without accompaniment, and never before had Lisa known her to play for guests. But her mother had asked for the cello to be brought downstairs, and Lisa had gotten it just before they sat down to dinner, while David leaned over the table pouring wine and Mrs. Armstrong added little notes to the recipe card she had written out for Elisabeth.

"Which of the many somber concerti?" her mother finally said, her voice hardly carrying into the kitchen, where Lisa poured hot boiled water down through a filter-lined cone, moving the kettle in a circle so that the water washed the dark coffee grounds toward the center. Her mother's voice had a peculiar quality about it, but Lisa was sure she recognized the emotional source of this tone. Many a time she had turned the corner into her mother's bedroom, the throaty resonances of the cello almost stalled in the air, holding, but resigned, sorrowful, and her mother's face washed with tears, her arms moving about the cello's body as though she were trying to comfort it, to embrace it without restricting it, her mother's hand holding the bow, the close tight movement, a hummingbird at honeysuckle, and then the long smooth draw of the bow across the strings and back again, and her other hand moving as a spider might move its articulated legs across a fingerboard, this fastidious movement at her mother's wet face held down close to the fingerboard, her head in its own visceral design of movement and response. "Don't go," she would say to Lisa. "Don't go," her voice above the low, sustained music of the cello. And then she would continue to play for a time as Lisa sat down on the carpet, her back leaning up against the cool wall, the reverent timbre of the music filling the room from the floor, from the ground, from some earthy cavern deep within the f-holes of the cello. "Don't ever go, baby."

She took the coffee to the living room and then returned to the kitchen. She snipped the string from a pink bakery box and lifted the cake David had brought from the flimsy paper flaps which spread across the counter like a stiff diaper or a cardboard bearskin. She recognized the bakery's hallmark: the great whimsical curls of white chocolate tinged pink sweeping up and around the cake as though it were a crown fashioned from flamingo feathers. She looked at the curls to see which might be picked off carefully enough so that others would not tumble after it and decided instead to insert a knife down through the swirl of one to bring up the champagne frosting to her mouth, where it melted across her tongue. She made sure the hole in the frosting was not detectable, slid the cake onto a platter, and walked with it to the living room, the sweet balm of the frosting still on her tongue.

The candles from the dining room were on the table alongside the coffeepot and cups. She settled the cake near the small plates and the forks and sat on the settee next to Mrs. Armstrong. Elisabeth sat across from them, the cello leaning back against her shoulder, the bow in her hand rising straight up from her knee. David walked in from the kitchen, and stood behind the settee, his pipe in his hand but no longer lit.

"Are we very ready for this *very* somber concerto?" Elisabeth asked, her hand at the peg board tightening a string. Lisa felt puzzled by the somewhat sarcastic looks exchanged between her mother and David.

"Should I cut this first?" she asked, reaching for the cake knife, the jumpy ambiance in the room unnerving her, making her want some activity to involve herself in.

"Nope. You can't do that just yet," David said. "You've got to sit through this piece first. Your mother's been working on it forever. No small amount of work has gone into this."

Her mother lowered the bow to the cello strings and played one long deep note and then three short notes. Lisa recognized "Happy Birthday" and started to laugh. She looked at David and her mother, but their faces were completely serious, completely engrossed in the slowest, most painful rendition of "Happy Birthday" she had ever heard.

"Oh God, do stop," Mrs. Armstrong said, laughing. "Here, let me pour coffee. Anything." But Elisabeth continued her long, slow playing until finally she dropped her head in mock acceptance of an imagined room full of thunderous applause. "For the love of God! Sing this child a decent 'Happy Birthday.' "

"None of us can sing, Mother," David said. "We thought this would *delight*, as it were."

"Delight what? Lisa, how do you put up with them?" Mrs. Armstrong asked.

"Your son here provided a birthday cake—impenetrable, I might add; you couldn't put a candle in the thing if you tried. We had to come up with something to replace the usual."

"Thanks, Mom," she said. She was relieved, and laughing because she was, though the image of her mother's face wet with tears lingered in the foreground of her mind, and lingering also in her mind's ear was the sound of the solo cello summoning from her mother the deep insatiable sadness. The candles glowed in the room; she continued to laugh; then the room was quiet except for her laughter, which sounded high and clattering—sounded like the glass of the door pane breaking out from its frame, the shards shattering against one another as they hit the floor, the shards clanking and tinkling as the door she was opening pushed them back against the cupboards.

"Now you can cut that cake," her mother said, putting the cello back in the corner. "We need a glass of hot water for the knife, though." Her mother was in the kitchen running the faucet, and then she returned, the glass on a folded towel in her hands, her face happy and relaxed, unconscious of the image she ghosted in her daughter's mind. "Okay, go at it. I don't envy you this task."

She dipped the knife blade in the hot water, drew it across the towel, and then held it poised above the crest of pink and white curls. She knew they were all looking at her, waiting on her, but she wanted to look at her cake a while longer, to see its high crown of smooth white chocolate and the pink tinges almost silvery in the candlelight.

"Do you know how those curls are made, Lisa?" Mrs. Armstrong asked, accepting the cup of coffee Elisabeth handed her. "I learned this the hard way," she continued; "I tried to do them at home by myself."

She was thinking of all the silly things she knew, and that at this moment she didn't want to hear yet something else; she didn't want to hear how chocolate was curled or which porcelain had this marque and which that; she wanted to know who was coming to dinner before it actually happened and whether her father and Mary were going to get married and whether or not David and her mother were lovers again and whether she had been born with a caul and what the dark

Lisa knew it was the call she had been expecting, though she had half expected him to call last night because of her birthday. But then again it would have had to come after he shaved in the morning, only then would he know his cologne was missing. She hesitated: he would want to know about next year. Her mother looked at her. And then she remembered he was in Canada, the scoped rifle against his shoulder, the moose quiet, unaware, dangerously humble. She took the receiver in her hand, the plastic light, almost buoyant.

After not hearing it for two years, his voice still sounded odd, far away, as though even if he was physically back in Sonoma his voice was still making the journey.

"Thank you for the birthday party last night—the cake and that unmentionable chrome object." They laughed together, his laughter in that ear cupped by the receiver and her own laughter ringing against the hard surfaces of the glassed-in porch.

"What are you two up to today?"

"I guess we're supposed to go shopping."

"You don't sound enthused. Shunning the avocation of your sex, are you?"

"Very funny." Her mother turned in her chair, a look of comfortable expectancy on her face. "I guess you want to talk to Mom. I'll—" She handed the receiver to her mother. "It's David." She moved to sit back down to finish her dish of bananas but the doorbell rang.

Through the glass panes along the side of the front door she could see two men in business suits. They both held briefcases and seemed unusually curious about the front garden, their eyes searching the beds along the porch and the urns planted with purple lobelia and pansies, which were now almost finished for the year.

"You have a lovely garden," one of the men said, turning back to Lisa with a smile that lingered for an unusually long time on his face.

"Thank you." There was another lengthy pause while the man smiled. She thought his body too close to the doorsill, as though he was a friend or someone she knew and it was just a matter of getting the door open before he was admitted. She finally said, "May I help you?" and was angered by having to ask something of them instead of the other way around.

"Sometimes people just don't take time enough to smell the roses," the man said, resuming his smile.

"That's what we'd like to talk to you about," the other man said, switching his briefcase to the other hand as though he was weary of carrying it, though this weariness did not manifest itself on his face or in his demeanor. She felt a subtle, covert pressure to let them in the house.

"I'm not sure I know what you want," she said.

"This is what they call a California pepper tree, isn't it?" the smiling man asked. "We had pepper trees where I come from but they didn't call them *California* pepper trees." She had the option of asking the man where he was from and thus starting a conversation or of continuing to probe the reason for his and his companion's presence on her front porch. The latter option seemed somehow rude and the former she didn't wish to pursue.

"When I was your age—"

"Hello, may I help you?" her mother asked the men, her voice forceful, almost mean.

"We were just wondering if your daughter here reads the Bible. And yourself? Do you read the Bible?"

"I'm sorry, I really don't have time to talk with you both."

"Yes, we keep finding that. No one has any time anymore. You don't have a couple of minutes right now, though? We'd just like to say a few things about the Lord, who gave us all this," he said, moving his open hand across the porch, gesturing toward the pepper tree and the house and the rose garden, which he could see through the pickets of the railing which enclosed the porch. "We tend to neglect what we should be most thankful—"

"I can't take this much presumption this early," Elisabeth said. "Thank you. Better luck elsewhere," and she shut the door with a shove which set the panes rattling nervously and the bolt into the jamb with a punchlike snap.

Lisa turned back into the living room. She felt a low, hot guilt; the men had seemed to her so earnest, guileless, in fact, because their presumption lacked novelty—lacked subtlety. She felt embarrassed for them, their suits and briefcases also—when she thought of it—guileless because that too was so obvious a ploy for respectability. They seemed to her the sort that one should be so careful not to offend, as though being rude to people of good intentions was a form of brutality.

"Maybe you shouldn't be so short with people like that," she said, hoping her mother would not turn one of her sudden angers upon her.

"Think God will smite us?" Elisabeth asked. "Think he'll ignite the big one over our transgressions?"

"I don't know, Mom. I just feel sorry for people like that. I mean, they don't intend any harm or anything; they're just doing what they think is right."

"Yes, but their implication by that 'rightness' is that I'm doing wrong. That form of judgment we can all do without."

"Are we going to do something with David?" she asked, the gray light of the porch strangely mean, this gray beginning to appear on the banana slices in the bowl at her place.

Her mother didn't look at her; she merely went on drinking her coffee, raising and lowering the cup, a cookbook spread on the table, the thick glossy pages buckling gently as her fingers reached them up and pushed them across. "Would you like to help David plant some things in his garden?" she asked finally. "He has some bulbs he wants in."

"Help David in his garden?" There was something oddly

incongruous about this suggestion, something about the tone in which it was made, as though it came in concert with the suggestion to lay the entire garden in cement. Of course, there was never any proof of this sort of duality in her mother's suggestions; it just seemed to be, much the way "pleased to meet you" is always at once true and not possibly true because how could you really know?

"I guess you impressed him with your gardening skills in Castro Valley. Has Mary put you under her tutelage?"

She took a deep breath and then began to answer her mother. "No. She tells me stuff, but she doesn't really—"

"Why does David think you're a gardener, then?" Elisabeth looked up from her book and smiled at her. "I think he knows something I don't know. How was your lunch with him anyway?"

"We went to a Japanese restaurant and had sushi. I liked it. I *think* I liked it." They both laughed.

"I hope he didn't make you eat anything *too* disgusting."

"I'm not quite sure." They both laughed again, the sound lingering, ringing softly against the windows and floor and table. "I didn't spit anything out, at any rate."

"I should hope not—"

"I was kidding, Mom," she said evenly. "You know I wouldn't do something like that."

"I know, baby—I know you wouldn't do that. I might, though."

"Oh, the truth! The truth emerges."

"God, I can't stand the stuff. Just can't abide it. What are we? Bears splashing around in a stream, dropping squiggling fish down our gullets?"

"I didn't know this about you. You never told me this."

"Very wise to keep your children in the dark about certain things—age, major dislikes. They get ideas."

"I guess that's why I never told you I liked to garden. Parents *really* get ideas. Entire weekends can fill up with one idea from a parent."

"Very funny."

"I thought so."

"I've spoiled you rotten. You've never had to do a lick of work in your life. Which is why I'm sending you off to slave in David's garden."

"Don't I get any say in this?" She put her hand on her mother's arm and jostled it back and forth playfully. "Come on, Mom. I wanna whine for a while first."

"Seriously, has Mary taught you some gardening? It's terrific if she has."

She was trying to steer clear of the subject of Mary. She thought of the news story about a motorcycle accident, the motorcycle going down because of a small leaf in the road, the leaf merely lying atop a spot of oil, the bike losing traction, sliding out from under its driver—Mary this leaf upon which an entire good afternoon could topple. "Wait a minute. What are you going to do if I go help David?" she asked.

"Practice. Does Mary—"

"Mom, I water when I'm there. I move the hose from one pot to another. Don't get ideas, I'm not a . . ." She stopped; she didn't want to hear the word "horticulturist" out loud, didn't want to hear the word "whore."

"Botanist. You're not a botanist."

SHE RODE HER BICYCLE to David's, taking a route that went up past the Sebastiani winery, the surfaced road becoming bumpier till what remained of pavement was merely small islands in an otherwise dirt road. Above her the sun cast down a scratchy net of heat. She looked at how golden her arms shone in the sunlight, that golden of wheat and wild grasses and the varnished weave of certain baskets, and of her father's cologne. She did not know why she had taken it, or how she would return it. She could feel the hard curve of the bicycle seat beneath her and the ridges of the rubber handlebar grips in her hands. A car sped past and she pulled her bicycle from the road to wait for the dust to settle, her waist and stomach leaning against the embrace of the handlebars. Horses grazed in a field and a sign wired to a fence with a hanger read: FRESH TOMATOES, CORN, BEANS. She looked behind her at the settling billows of dust and up the hillside at the burned-out hull of a stone house, the sirens as loud in her head on this day as they were that early morning she stood on the back porch looking through the condensation on the windows at the fire swelling from the hill in lead-gray clouds streaked with gold and red.

She had to decide about next year, or perhaps not so much decide as stave off any thoughts of Castro Valley—any thoughts of changing the situation of her custody, that balance achieved across the years not because it was balance but because it was that crabbed equilibrium which time and fate sooner or later achieve regardless of intention or principle—achieve the way a plant tucked away will twist and gnarl its way toward the sun, its pot never moved, its trunk skewed far from its base but somehow balanced, static.

She stood her weight on the high pedal, moving the bicycle off down the road, in her mind in these initial moments of pushing off—always and every time—the fearful glimmer of falling open-legged against the green crossbar.

"DO YOU WANT SOME GLOVES?" he was asking her, his face turned down into a box of stakes and trowels and half-used bags of potting soil. "Here. Use these." He passed her a pair of flowered gloves stiff with patches of dried mud. "Those must be my mother's."

The yard looked dry—tremendously unhappy, she thought. There was a mulch of rotting fruit beneath a plum tree; it smelled of moist earth and vinegar. Rosebushes profuse with the rust-brown tufts of past blooms crawled the back fence, and the bricked planter beds—once impressionistic with azaleas and rhododendrons, and in the spring with lilies and tulips and narcissi—were now cracked dry from lack of water and care. The brown hulls of the rhododendrons stood stark and delineated like a lithograph of winter, or of war. She pulled on Mrs. Armstrong's gloves. They fit her hands perfectly, and this pleased her, as though—just for an instant— she could have Mrs. Armstrong's unhurried confidence, her fine, schooled voice, the ready humor and stories. She rubbed her gloved hands together and the dirt crumbled off onto the brick walk in a soft patter.

"I don't understand why you haven't at least watered back here." She struggled to subdue the accusation in her voice. "It seems some of this could be saved."

"Go to it, Clara Barton; the hose is over there."

How many weeks had David been home, she wondered, three, four? Enough, even if he had spent the last two with her mother—something she didn't know for sure, but which seemed now in this dry, untended yard more than likely. Elisabeth did want him; he was wrong—had misunderstood her, and the garden they were about to rejuvenate stood for that arid period of misunderstanding, that period of time he was in the desert, that time that would soon be no longer. She walked to the hose reel near the back door of the house and pulled the hose by its nozzle down the brick path to the roses. David turned the water on and the gray dirt began to darken and lift.

"I've gotten a mass of bulbs to put in," he said. "We may be putting in some too early, but, as you say, something needs to be done back here." He pulled his shirt off, his back arching, his head ducking, and threw it down across an iron chair. He was thin, with little or no musculature, and she found him beautiful in that way that very thin dogs are beautiful, whippets and greyhounds and borzois, a type of fleshlessness which seemed otherworldly, taut and driven and fine and remote.

They soaked the flower beds till the thin branches and stumps of the azaleas and rhododendrons could be pulled up, the clumps of root and wet soil like the beards of great men, of Moses and Tolstoy, and of Rasputin, though she supposed Rasputin hadn't been great, only irrepressible, unkillable. David knapped the clods against his tennis shoe, the dark soil falling away only slightly, the beards intact, heavy and leaden and thrown together into the metal garbage can like so many heads within a grave. Then he turned the soil with a shovel, mixing the earth with peat and fertilizer and a soil conditioner of redwood which smelled of the sequoia forest—that high smell the trees, their bark, had on a damp winter day. She went down the planter beds with a bulb dibble, making row after row, hole after hole, and then they sat together reading the thatch of cardboard at the top of each netted bag of bulbs: the gladiolas would get this tall and so should be down the middle, the irises would grow this high and so should go there, daffodils would go here nicely and tulips here and lilies of the valley and paper-whites and crocuses there. Into the narrow holes they settled the bulbs, the tiny padding of roots at the bottom, the elfish point of stalk at the top. She took her gloves off so that she could feel the smooth, crackling scale leaves of the bulb. From this small, pinched, brown onion of a sphere would spring tall, narrow swords of green, one sword embedded in another embedded in another embedded in another till, guarded enough, a stalk of flowers would rise up from inside the several hilts, a stalk of violet and snow, one of golden trumpets, and another of white stars alight in the center with the fine yellow powder of pollen. She realized he watched her as she patted down the last mound of soil and shredded red bark, watched her mottled fingers tamp the dirt into the hole and then into a small peak vaguely reminiscent of the bulb's top.

"Come on. Let's get cleaned up," he said, slapping her gloves together to rid them of dirt. He tossed them back into the box of trowels and stakes. She looked at them there, slouched haphazard, discarded; she would have smoothed their fingers and laid them evenly across the bags of potting soil. She turned away.

"Do you think the roses will survive?" she asked.

"Probably. They might not bloom so much next year, but they're pretty hearty once they get that old."

"Where'd you learn to garden?" She ran the nail of her baby finger under her other nails to clean them, each soiled nail once again a pale crescent; "a thumbnail moon," Mary had called the deep white sickle in the black sky one night.

"I didn't. I know a little from my mother. She loves roses. Those at the house are probably fifty years old, if not older." He dragged the metal garbage can along the walk and then stopped. "What are you thinking about? Suddenly you're gone."

"A lamb I once saw." The screech of the garbage can against the brick still rang in her ear. "At a circus."

"Go on—"

"I don't know what made me think of it. The roses surviving, I guess. 'Drought resistance' "—it was a phrase of Mary's.

"I'm still lost."

"It was a two-headed lamb in a cage. A wagon, really, that had bars. And I asked my father if it would still have two heads when it grew up and he said it would die soon, that it was like mentally retarded people, that it wouldn't live long."

She looked at him, at his face glistening in the sun and then back down at her muddy hands. "I don't know why I thought of it."

"You always want reasons." He resumed dragging the garbage can to the side of the house. "Come on," he beckoned. He held the back door for her. She felt self-conscious walking toward him, a fine powder of dirt tickling her face, streaks of mud on her arms and legs and hands. "Come here." He pulled her to the kitchen sink and held her hands under the faucet; she could smell the earthy wet-wool redolence of his sweat. The screen door clattered shut just as she let escape a whimper, his long fingers rubbing too roughly against the pale gashes on her right hand. "I'm sorry. I forgot."

She pulled her hands from his. "I can do it, I'm sure."

He yanked a towel from the side of the refrigerator and slung it across the counter. "There's something for you by the telephone." She glanced over at the package wrapped in ribbed brown paper and tied with string. It looked old-fashioned, something a shopkeeper would wrap for a Dickens character, a round of cheese or a meter of cloth. The towel felt harsh against her skin but she rubbed briskly anyway. "I'll be right back," he said.

He was in the shower, the hum of the water in the walls. She sat at a small wooden table in the living room and drew her foot across the floor, stopping at the fringe of a rug he had probably brought from Saudi. She rested her hand on the package. There was the squeak and thump of the pipes and almost immediately he stood before her in a towel, beads of water covering his body, and then a trail of water, a path of clear flat stones, across the floor and rug to the stereo.

"You haven't opened that yet? Open it." He threaded the end of a tape onto a reel, his finger then rotating the reel till the shiny ribbon became taut. He didn't seem bothered about the water on the floor or—she supposed—the chill of bath water on one's body when it is not quickly toweled off. She pulled the end of the string and it slackened its hold on the brown paper, which expanded and rose as though it were a round of dough.

"I didn't know if you would grow or not."

It was a short black garment rather like a smock but with a tie at the neck instead of buttons. Embroidered up and down its front and across the back were designs of brown and gold and blue. She couldn't decide what they were, perhaps leaves or stylized camels. She held it up but not against herself because of the dirt and mud. The fabric was strangely heavy, perhaps a particularly thick crepe, but she wasn't sure.

"It's Bedouin," he said distractedly, his fingers holding the reels lightly as they began to rotate. "They're nomadic—although not quite so much as they once were. Do you like it?"

"I'm not sure—I mean, yes, of course I like it, but it seems mysterious, spooky—"

"Exotic."

"No, it's too heavy to be exotic." She heard the first strains of Elgar; she looked up; he was once again watching her.

"Elgar," she said, as though his watching had wanted an answer.

"Yes, but which?" He smiled, amused, happy.

"Do you play this game with my mother?" she said. She folded the black garment atop the paper it had been wrapped in.

There was a slow beat between them. "No, I don't play this game with your mother," he said angrily. He pulled a chair from beneath the table and sat down. "I don't want . . ." He paused. He looked out the front windows of the house, his hair as dark and as wet as the soil they had just planted. "I—" he began again.

"It doesn't matter, though, does it? Because you'll just go along with them."

"Who? You mean your parents?" He got up abruptly and walked down the hall to his bedroom. He returned wearing shorts, pulling a shirt over his head, his back still beaded with water from his shower, and then his back covered, the shirt darkening slightly from the moisture.

"We always talk like this," she said. "About nothing. About everything."

"Do you always push like this?"

"I'm not pushing—"

He walked past her to the kitchen. "You don't even know when you're pushing, you don't even know what I'm talking about." She heard the kiss of the refrigerator door closing and a jar being set down on the tile. "You don't even know what you're pushing for, do you?"

Trucks rumbled in the distance on the way to the Haraszthy winery. She thought of cycling there, alone, down the lane of eucalyptus trees, their trunks as furled and frayed as that old-time twine used in hardware or feed stores. She wanted to pass under the stone edifice into the winery dug years ago in the mountain by Chinese laborers with kitchen spoons, the cave ceilings a firmament of small ovals where hour after hour the spoons had fed on the dank soil. She wanted to go there and stand in the darkness, in the smell of new wine, and in the caves dripping with their subterranean nectar which—if she listened closely enough, fancifully enough—she could hear striking the huge casks, the moisture bleeding into the oak, runneling its way through the grain to the small grotto of wine within. She wanted this sharp dark coolness, and to be here in the noon warmth, with David.

"Don't tease," he said. She could feel her jaw tightening, the teeth moving in upon themselves the way a sea anemone constricts. "And if you do, you better know what you're teasing for."

"I merely said, 'Do you play'—"

"Do you know someone named Bill?" he asked. "Tall guy." With a long spoon he scooped olives out of a jar and into a bowl. "Maybe plays basketball; hangs around."

"What do you mean, hangs around?"

"Ah, so the name does ring a bell—"

"How do *you* know him?" She watched him slice a loaf of French bread along its narrow length, the knife sawing slowly beneath the palm of his hand.

"I don't, I just know he's an admirer of yours."

She supposed he thought this news would please her, but with mud daubed along her arms and legs and the fine layer of dirt on her face, it maddened her, as though Bill had suddenly, actually, been brought into the room and stood above her, looking down on her as though she were the gardening gloves, discarded and untidy. "You sound like a wall in the girls' bathroom at school: Bill likes Lisa."

"Tell me about him."

"What do you mean, tell you about him?"

"What's he like . . . other than you?" He buttered the bread halves, the knife cracking against the butter dish every time he sliced off a curl of butter.

"He's a very good mathematician."

"Yeah? That's interesting . . . what else?"

"What else? Nothing else. I barely know him." She thought of telling him to leave the butter out of the fridge so that it would be easier to spread, but she didn't.

"Seems he knows you. You want to clean up?"

"You haven't told me how you know him."

"Why don't you give the guy a chance—"

"A chance at what, David?"

"You know what I mean. Come on, he's a good guy—he likes you. And he's the right age."

"What does that matter—that only makes it worse," she hissed.

"What?" But David couldn't understand, couldn't see her bedroom dappled with origami animals, or her mother's script across the belly of a blue chicken: "Was blue, missed you,

cock-a-doodle-doo blue, Achoo, God bless you, you're home!"
He couldn't see the cardboard table in her old bedroom, or
the momentary dark cast in Mary's eyes when she'd pulled
back too soon from hugging her—you had to love somebody
well. Or not at all.

"How do you know Bill? How do you know if he's a good
guy?" When she spoke, her jaw felt shot through with quills.
Her voice sounded gravelly. He folded ham slices and patted
them down onto ruffles of lettuce.

"I don't, I just overheard a conversation at Lynch's while
I waited for a prescription for my mother. He was defending
you—I heard them call him Bill. And he just looked like a
basketball player—a little too tall, a little too slender, close-
cut hair."

"What was he defending me for?"

"I gather that you're aloof—"

"You mean 'stuck-up,' they wouldn't use the word 'aloof.' "

"God, you are so bloody cynical."

She walked to the bathroom. David's razor lay on the glass
counter with two oval brushes and a pot of shaving cream.
They had a smooth austerity that seemed particularly masculine to her, the objects specific and simple and obvious—
not mascara or compacts whose presence implied both that
you could look better and that you also needed to look better,
a cipher that buoyed as it drowned. She turned the hot-water
faucet on, rotating it as far as it would turn, droplets of water
raining up onto the mirror.

"Hungry?" he called to her, his voice muted and far away,
though there were no longer the great sandy reaches of Saudi
between them. She moved to twist the lock in place, to close
herself into the bathroom as she had done so many times
before, the cool tile around her, the loud noiselessness of the
running water a type of shroud. She could feel deep in her
pelvis the high hot sting of her bladder, and in her mind the

burning question—"your father's fantasy," her mother called it—of next year.

She looked up toward the sash window, one gray streaked pane raised behind the other, and in the glass chamber the two panes made, the light caught and lingered.

Steam rose up the mirror in an arch; she turned the faucet off, the water funneling down the drain—leaving—and then completely gone with one loud happy chortle. There were two years before her, she thought, not just next year; there was the year about to begin, and the one after that. Perhaps she could spend this year in Castro Valley and come back her senior year to Sonoma. A year with her father and a year with her mother, this year away better because then she could come back and be with her mother, and David was here now too and he could be with Elisabeth, and David could miss her and feel bad—and she, Lisa, would be the one leaving—and her father could have his time, the time Mary said he wanted; this seemed reasonable, promising, an acceptable solution.

She dampened the washcloth and pulled it up her legs, the water cooling on her thighs, drawing her skin up into a thousand tiny mounds. She washed her face and arms and then sat on the edge of the tub, the coldness through her shorts like the night her mother and she had first arrived in Sonoma and sat on the back stoop eating apples and cheese, the damp cement seeping through to their bones, moving them to rise up the stairs to the sleeping bags laid side by side in the pearly glimmer of the vacant house.

"Well, is it true? Are you stuck-up?" he asked as she came into the kitchen. "These kids know what they're talking about?"

She felt that lingering sadness which shadowed and deepened the present but which had little to do with it. She didn't even really know what they meant—what they thought or talked about or cared about. She felt very far away from them

all. They disliked her, made fun of her. She could feel herself
falling, could feel some composite figure beating her with a
cudgel, beating her head and then her face and shoulders, her
body sagging into itself, the dense dull thud of the club hitting
her. Then she sat in her barn, under its high, drafty roof—
she was leaving them all. She clutched the edge of the kitchen
counter.

"I'm sorry, I didn't mean to make you cry."

"I'm not crying," but then she felt the cold hotness of tears
down her cheeks. "It has nothing to do with you, anyway."

"Come on. I want you to eat something. I called your mom.
She's coming over."

On the counter he set a plate before her overhung on both
sides by sandwich. He reached across and scratched the top
of her head. "Come on, what do you want to drink? Milk?
Water?" His hand slid from her head down her temple to her
cheek, where it hovered, and then slowly dropped. He looked
for a moment sad, but caught himself, or seemed to. She could
still feel his hand.

"I can't eat all this; I'm not a horse," she said.

"Ah, good, we've ruled out two things today—you're not
stuck-up and you're not a horse. Anything else we can rule
out?" She wanted to tell him it wasn't funny, that nothing was
funny, that laughing was a moment off guard and that someday
he would pay for that unwatched instant, but she laughed
anyway, awkwardly, feeling in this moment of relaxation her
face aching with the strain of vigilance.

"Stop it. I'd like a glass of water, please." Her grip relaxed
on the counter and she bent from the waist and rested on her
elbows.

"Why don't you just demand a glass of water—just say, 'I
want a glass of water, period.' Just come right out and demand
it."

She laughed again, louder, David thought this could all be

easier than it was, could all be mastered with insistence, with putting your foot down—with knowing what you wanted. He scratched her head again. She read in his face, "She's a good kid, she can be humored, can be cajoled into happier moods." Of course, she thought to herself, of course she could. What could possibly surprise them about that? "Give me a glass of water or I'll shoot!" she announced. They both giggled, the sound of the faucet turning on and off as he got her the water.

"What are you two laughing about?" Elisabeth stood looking through the screen of the back door. She was smiling, her hands tucked in at her waist. "Looks good out here. Or it will come spring."

Neither of them answered. She looked down at the huge sandwich stretched across the plate. "Do you have a knife?" she asked quietly. "I think we can cut this in two. Mom, are you hungry?" she said louder, raising her head.

"I made that entire thing for you, you horse," he whispered, but she didn't laugh.

"Thank you."

"Beer, Elisabeth?" he said as she came into the kitchen.

"I'd love one." He flipped the cap off a bottle with a church key and handed it to her; Lisa liked that name, "church key," which she supposed was irreverent, though it seemed to have lost the ability to offend. It was only its triangular shape that gave rise to the church part of it, to the Trinity—that's what her father had told her. It was all in the end rather innocent really, though something in her wanted it to remain risqué, on the edge, every time you used it, a bit naughty, a bit sacrilegious.

In the garden, on the iron chairs warmed by the sun, they sat and ate the ham and butter sandwiches. She didn't think that she had ever had a sandwich made with butter instead of mayonnaise; it had a different, more subtle taste, and the lettuce without the lubricant of mayonnaise lingered on her tongue, waxy and rather dry. In her nostrils was the peppery smell of the moist dirt drying in the heat. The French bread crust abraded the roof of her mouth; she put her sandwich down and didn't eat any more.

"So, what did you put where?" Elisabeth asked, bending to reach under her chair for her beer. "You put in some crocuses? Because they'll bloom early."

"We put in everything, glads, crocuses, tulips, daffs—"

"Daffs? You learn that from Mary?" She groaned and rolled her eyes, but then her face lifted into laughter. "Daffs!"

"What's wrong with 'daffs,' Elisabeth?" He looked down at the ground and then kicked a pebble across the brick with his bare toe. "Did you know that your daughter has an admirer?"

"Cut it out, David."

"No, I'm not kidding, a real honest-to-God admirer, one who wears her scarf into battle."

"What are you—"

"Chivalric code—"

"Platonic," her mother said under her breath.

"What, Mom?" She watched Elisabeth tuck her beer bottle beneath her chair again.

"I said if you find one of those, you better keep him."

"You said something else—"

"I said, it's platonic."

"It isn't always platonic, Elisabeth—let's hope not," David said, rising and walking over to the plum tree, the placement of his bare feet particular so as not to step on the scattered tree falls. He reached up into the tree, his hands disappearing into the foliage, the leaves rustling like a taffeta slip. She looked around the yard and then over her shoulder at the bathroom window. The sun had tinned the glass into a sheet of flashing and the light caught and flickered at the corner of her eye.

"You want another beer, Elisabeth?" he asked, turning around to face them.

"Oh, why not."

He dropped the plums into Lisa's hands as he walked past and in through the kitchen door. They were small smooth spheres ripened and dark with sun. The fruit felt sensuous to her fingertips, the soft balm of flour in a canister which you have lowered your hands into.

"Mom?"

"Hmm . . ."

"How'd your practicing go?" She leaned forward and poured all but one of the plums into her mother's lap.

"I found something in your room, Lisa."

"There are lots of things in my room—"

"Neville's after-shave."

"It's not after-shave, Mom. He doesn't use after-shave—he uses an electric shaver—it's cologne."

"What are you up to?"

"I'm not *up* to anything." The "up" came out low and hard, several registers beneath the sound of the screen door slapping shut. David handed Elisabeth a beer.

"What are you two whispering about?" he asked.

"Nothing." She felt a trickle of juice travel across her wrist and down the inside of her thigh; the plum pulp pushed out between her fingers.

"Neville's after-shave," her mother said. "It seems we now own a whole bottle of the stuff." They both seemed amused. David sat back down and propped his feet against the planter box.

"Well, I suppose that's appropriate now that she's taken up shaving." They laughed aloud this time. She could feel the sharp ridge of the plum's pit in her palm.

"About next year." She spoke quickly. This was not the right time—it was the worst in fact, and unfair to her mother—but she wanted to deflate the airy loft of their laughter, to see their faces fall, not into sadness but into thought. "Why don't I go to Castro Valley this year and then come back here next

year. It seems it would be fair that way—a year in both places—
and I'd be back then too. Don't you think that would be fair,
Mom?"

"That's what you're up to?" she asked, her face surprised,
still half laughing, but the answer to her own question known
in her eyes darkening with tears.

"I'm not *up* to anything—I'm not sneaking around." She
looked across at David. He gazed downward, into his lap.

"Did David help you with this scheme? Is that why you're
bringing this up now—because David's here?"

"I'm not sure it's a scheme, Elisabeth—"

"I thought you were happy to be home—I thought you
wanted—"

"I don't think that's the issue," David said. "I think it has
to do—"

"I didn't ask you what the issue was, David, I asked my
daughter."

She looked at her mother, at the smooth rise of her cheeks.
"Mom, why don't we talk about this later; David had nothing
to do with anything. I made the decision myself—I was trying
to be fair."

"Fair. Don't use abstractions when you don't know what
they mean." Elisabeth stood up quickly and the plums dropped
from her lap onto the brick. She swiped at the tears on her
face. "And why, Lisa, if you don't want to talk about this now,
did you bring it up? Do you feel a safety with David here, is
that it? Is that fair?" She kicked at the plums near her feet.
"You can use this time, but I can't?"

"You're right, this wasn't the right time. I'm sorry."

"But timing's not exactly the point," David began. "What
about—"

"No. That's *what about*. She's not going off to live with her
father while he's shacked up with some gardener."

"But that's not the point either, is it, Elisabeth?" He said this calmly, his legs still stretched out and resting on the planter box.

"David, I made a mistake. Mom's right."

"You might have made a mistake, but I didn't. Can't you see this, Lisa? Can't you see? Why do you have your father's after-shave? Huh? Why? Think about it."

"I don't know, I just do." She stood up and looked down into David's calm face. "What does it matter anyway? I just took it."

"Don't get angry at me, Lisa, get angry at your mother."

"Let's go, sweetheart."

"I'm not angry at my mother, I'm angry at you." Elisabeth started toward the walk along the side of the house.

"No you're not, you're angry at your mother—"

"I am not."

"Stick to architecture, David," Elisabeth said over her shoulder and disappeared.

"Why'd you do that?" She didn't wait for an answer but hurried down the walk. Her right hand was covered in pulp and between her fingers were strips of purple-black plum skin like wisps of eel.

"Aren't you going to take your gift?" David called. "It's been waiting to go home with you for a long time now." She kept walking as though she hadn't heard him. She rounded the corner onto the front lawn. It crunched with dryness and did not give to the step the way a green, well-watered yard would have. The engine of the Mercury roared and her mother pulled the column shift down into gear and drove off. She felt mean, the plum pulp sealing her fingers together, the sharp ridge of the pit in her palm, and the lawn hard beneath her feet. Stooping, she wiped her hand on the stiff bristle of grass. It surrounded her, this immense scrub brush, working at the bottoms of her sneakers, and now between its bristles was the plum pit, was the gray-orange pulp and the school of wispy eels.

"Hey—" David stood behind her. "Come back and eat your lunch."

"Why'd you do that?"

"It's a small town, but I'll handle it." He pulled her by the shoulders. "Come on." They walked back along the path. The leaves of an ivy vine fingered her arm as they passed.

"There's something between you and Mom."

"No. There hasn't been something between us for a long time. I told you that. There is, however, something between you and Elisabeth."

"Of course there is, she's my—"

"I don't mean that. I mean me." The sun was behind him and she couldn't look up into his face. "I'm between you two."

"You put your nose in—you did that."

"We were just teasing you about the after-shave—"

"You tell me not to tease but you both can do it."

"Different type of teasing, Lisa, you know that—"

"I don't know anything. You're always talking as if I know exactly what you mean. I don't. What's different about them?"

"One's sexual. You know that." As though she'd inhaled deeply from a bottle of bleach, a swift hot pain rose up through her nostrils behind her eyes, filling her temples and mind. "Me, in order to get to her. You know I'm right."

It seemed as though several minutes passed before she could finally speak again. "You're not right, David. Whatever you think, you're wrong. I do like you, I really do." She sounded ridiculous to herself, her saliva bitter in her mouth and burning her chest as she swallowed. "I don't have a plan like you seem to think—would it be this messed up if I did?" He picked the top off her sandwich and started pulling it apart and tossing it out into the garden. The pieces fell on the freshly planted bulbs, some tumbling down the small moist peaks. She looked at the slice of ham in the sunlight; it seemed as though it was the pink flesh of gums.

"No, maybe not."

A group of sparrows gathered and pecked at the big jagged crumbs. Their heads dipped down and sprang back, mechanistic, the jerk of ratchets and springs and reflexes. He stacked the three plates, the remainder of her sandwich left on top, and walked in the back door.

"I have to go," she said. Her voice sounded polite, and cold.

"I was surprised you were lingering." She followed him in the house and then lifted her sandwich off the plate just as he lowered it into the sink.

"Do you have a paper towel, or a napkin?" He ripped a towel off a roll beneath the sink and handed it to her. She folded it carefully around the sandwich; it seemed precious to her, this food, half of which had been fed to tiny brown creatures nervous as eyelids.

"Why now?"

"Why now what?" She walked to the living room and grabbed up the black smock. She left the heavy paper it had been wrapped in on the table.

"Why—all of a sudden—are you going to eat something?"

"You're very brilliant about why I do things—you figure it out."

"I'm sorry, Lisa."

"Don't apologize to me—I'm just a—just a—tart or something—remember?"

"Hey—"

"Hey." She pushed out through the screen door and rounded the corner of the house to where her bicycle stood.

"Thank you for helping with the garden," he called after her. She didn't want to say thank you for the Bedouin smock. She pushed the seat of her bicycle away from her and booted the kickstand back. It snapped smartly. It wasn't very graceful to leave without a word—it wasn't elegant at all. A thick cable stretched from the roof of her mouth down into her body; it held her words taut, unspoken. The tires of her bicycle made a clicking sound as they rolled across the brick.

SHE DIDN'T KNOW WHAT TIME it was, two perhaps or three. She rode her bicycle to the Sebastiani winery and then started up the hill away from Spain Street. In one hand she clutched her sandwich, and in the other, the heavy black fabric with its blue and gold embroidery. Only her baby fingers hooked down around the handlebar grips and steered. She wasn't angry at her mother, she just wanted her to understand, to see that going to live with her father for a year was fair. She reached the railroad tracks that ran behind the wheat field and started down them, her walk a type of goose step so that her foot could land each time on a tie and not in the gravelly ballast between. She had forgotten the plum juice on her thigh, but now it caught her other thigh and held it, the skin glued together, and then pulled apart with her step to another tie, and then stuck together again, and pulled apart. She balanced her bicycle on one rail and the rubber tires squealed against the burnished steel. The rails were anvils, continuous, squat, narrow anvils, running on either side of her and before her into the curve of pepper trees and straight behind her as far she could see into the distant wavy heat. She could hear the ring of hammers pounding the anvils, a steady metronomic pounding.

She reached the barn and lifted her bicycle down off the rail. Just as she had left it two weeks earlier, a wooden crate held the barn door closed. It swung wide when she pulled the crate back and wheeled her bicycle in between a buckboard and the body of an old pie wagon. She looked to the back of the barn to where she had her desk made of crates. It was there, untouched, the jug of leaves and the jar with pencils very still in the streaked light. She turned around and looked over the railroad tracks out across the wheat field to the house. The Mercury stood in the carport. She pushed the door open wider so that she could see more of the porch windows from the inside of the barn. She wasn't exactly sure what she wanted to see; perhaps Elisabeth would walk down the road and get her, would say she understood and that two years split fairly down the middle. David, she knew, would not come because he didn't know about the barn. Of course, maybe her mother had told him, maybe he would come and hold her cheek in his hand.

On the buckboard she sat cross-legged for a while and then lay down along the ridged, dry wood very carefully so that she wouldn't get splinters. She rolled the thick black Bedouin fabric into a pillow. It felt cool against her neck in the static, dusty heat of the barn. She held her sandwich up over her head and looked at it; oil from the ham had darkened the paper toweling. In the eaves there was the rustle and flutter of birds. She thought of feeding them the rest of the bread from her sandwich but then sat back up and placed it before her. She unfolded the towel and pressed it down flat. It had two serrated edges and two smooth edges. Picking up the sandwich, she turned the paper towel over so that the design of blue cornucopia showed. She put the sandwich down and then folded the serrated edges under; she thought it almost a plate with a blue-and-white pattern. With the ham peeled off and put to one corner, the lettuce to another and the bread to another, she had a three-course meal and she ate slowly, the ham salty and smooth on her tongue, the bread bland, comforting, and the lettuce tasting of minerals and of the earth in the hot catalyzing sun.

She made herself think of her mother eating dinner alone at the table on the porch—made herself see the candles casting one huge solitary shadow against the white surface of the back cupboards. She had to get used to this thought, this image;

she had to think about it as much as possible in order to get over it, around it; yesterday she had vowed to preserve her mother's happiness, and today she had destroyed it. She made herself hear the sound of the turning pages of the book her mother would read; she forced herself to imagine her mother's plate rather sloppily dished up because now Elisabeth didn't need to bother—didn't care to bother; she insisted she see her mother decorating the Christmas tree, or eating Thanksgiving dinner, the roast turkey on the table before her, the one slice taken off its breast looking as though it were merely an abrasion, a tiny scrape; she saw the kitchen towel in her mother's lap because Elisabeth didn't care to use a pressed napkin just for herself—she heard the creak of her mother's solitary footsteps in the kitchen and on the stairs—she heard the rip of Scotch tape as Elisabeth took down each piece of origami, the many elephants, the cranes, the frogs and lobsters, and the seal with its forked tail; the next time she came home, it wouldn't be like yesterday, it wouldn't be a celebration—it would merely be evidence that she had made a choice and gone away, a bright caravan of paper animals following.

She looked down at the paper towel spread before her. It wasn't a square, and for origami you needed a square, she knew that much. She made the towel square by folding one edge in and then tearing it carefully along the crease. Then she folded it in triangles, then unfolded it so that now—spread out—the creases were spokes, a square wheel, a pane of glass cracked from some central impact, the tires of her father's car framed by her window, her mother's car boxed by the carport at the corner of the field of wheat and sunflowers, the square wheel beneath her fingertips being moved, folded, crumpled up into a ball and tossed, its soundless arc of flight and then the buoyant roll across the dirt of the barn.

She needed to make a list of things to do. She took the narrow strip of paper towel and jumped down from the buckboard; somewhere a metal chain knocked against wood. At her desk, she pulled a pencil from the jar and started to write, but because of the oil from the ham, the gray lead showed only here and there, as though the list were in shadows. Call Mary; pack; cologne; talk to Mother.